SAND

OTHER BOOKS FOR YOUNG READERS
BY LUANNE ARMSTRONG

Morven and the Horse Clan
(Great Plains Press, 2013)

I'll Be Home Soon
(Ronsdale Press, 2012)

Pete's Gold
(Ronsdale Press, 2008)

Into the Sun
(Hodgepog Books, 2002)

Jeannie and the Gentle Giants
(Ronsdale Press, 2001)

Maggie and Shine
(Hodgepog Books, 1999)

Arly and Spike
(Hodgepog Books, 1997)

Annie
(Polestar Press, 1995)

Sand

Luanne Armstrong

RONSDALE PRESS

SAND

RONSDALE PRESS
3350 West 21st Avenue, Vancouver, B.C., Canada V6S 1G7
www.ronsdalepress.com

Typesetting: Julie Cochrane, in Minion 12 pt on 16
Cover Design: Nancy de Brouwer
Paper: Ancient Forest Friendly "Silva" (FSC) — 100% post-consumer waste,
    totally chlorine-free and acid-free

Ronsdale Press wishes to thank the following for their support of its publishing
program: the Canada Council for the Arts, the Government of Canada through the
Canada Book Fund, the British Columbia Arts Council, and the Province of British
Columbia through the British Columbia Book Publishing Tax Credit program.

Library and Archives Canada Cataloguing in Publication

Armstrong, Luanne, 1949–, author
    Sand / Luanne Armstrong.

Issued in print and electronic formats.
ISBN 978-1-55380-473-4 (print)
ISBN 978-1-55380-474-1 (ebook) / ISBN 978-1-55380-475-8 (pdf)

    I. Title.

PS8551.R7638S26 2016   jC813'.54   C2016-902125-4   C2016-902126-2

At Ronsdale Press we are committed to protecting the environment. To this end we
are working with Canopy and printers to phase out our use of paper produced from
ancient forests. This book is one step towards that goal.

Printed in Canada by Marquis Printing, Quebec

*Dedicated with deepest
gratitude to Christine Ross,
Michelle Whiteaway and all the
other caring people at the
Creston and District Therapeutic
Riding Centre*

ACKNOWLEDGEMENTS

I would like to thank Robin Armstrong,
Avril Woodend, Dorothy Woodend,
Geronimo Morris, Joanne Gailius
and Christine Ross for their care,
support, and comments.

Chapter 1

SHE WOKE IN THE DARK. She tried to move but something was holding her arms and legs. She tried to call out but something was blocking her throat. She couldn't see. She shook her head from side to side. Fear shot through her body. Then gradually her eyelids lifted. A dim grey light sifted in. It felt as if her eyelids were stuck together. She wanted to rub them but couldn't. When she shook her head, she grew dizzy. The world swam around her. A terrible pain in her back and arms cascaded into her waking mind.

And then a voice, cool, distant. "Are you awake? Just nod your head if you can hear me."

Such a relief. Someone who would help her. She nodded

her head. A hand on her wrist, her shoulder. Noise. Beeping. Where was she?

"Do you know where you are?"

She shook her head, but slowly. Her head didn't want to move. Pain lanced through her forehead.

"You're in the hospital. You can't talk because there is a tube in your throat, helping you breathe. Do you remember anything?"

Her memory was blank. She shook her head again.

"That's okay. That's normal," said the voice. "You've been sleeping for a couple of days. You were in a car accident. You hit your head and hurt your back and some other things. Now I am going to call the doctor and see if I can get permission to take the tube out of your throat so you can talk. Can you lie still until I get back?"

She nodded. She could hear footsteps moving away. No, don't go, she wanted to say but couldn't. She could hear other things now as well. Other machines, beeping. A fan, blowing air. Distant voices. She lay still until she could hear voices, coming closer. A man's voice, a woman's voice. The pain came and went in waves, but she couldn't scream, couldn't say anything or ask for help.

The pain came back and built in a wave. She started to shake and then a man's voice said, "Well, well, how are we feeling? Better? No, don't try to talk. We'll get the tube out and call your parents to let them know you're awake. Now just lie back and try to relax. Breathe normally."

He put a hand on her shoulder, then leaned on her chest. He was choking her!

She hated this man. How could she breathe when he was leaning on her chest and choking her? Relax? Was he crazy? When she was in so much pain?

And then the tube slid out of her throat and she could breathe again and the pain slid away as well and the man was gone. Time was doing funny things.

"Now," the woman said — was she a nurse? — a doctor? "I am going to put some drops in your eyes to help you open them."

The drops helped to clear the grey fuzziness that had been hindering her sight and now, finally, she could see. Yes, a hospital room, a nurse in green scrubs. A tube sending fluids into her arm, one of the things that hurt. Windows. Outside the windows it was dark.

"What time is it?" she croaked.

"It's three a.m., Tuesday morning. You had your accident on Saturday afternoon. So you've been asleep for a while. Now, dear, what is your name?"

Her name? Why would the nurse ask her such a stupid question? Didn't they know her name? Come to think of it, what was her name? She tried to concentrate. Shouldn't she know her own name? Finally, it filtered into her mind from a long, grey distance away.

"Willy," she croaked. Even her voice didn't work properly. "Willa Cameron. I live in Redfish, British Columbia. My parents are Elizabeth and Donald Cameron. I have a sister, and her name is . . . Emily." She felt quite triumphant after this and exhausted as well.

"Good," said the nurse briskly. "Very well done. Now, I want you to try and rest. I am going to call your parents and let them know you are awake. It will take them a little while to get here. They're in a hotel a few blocks away. Are you in pain? Just nod if you are and I'll give you something for it."

She nodded, hard. But she had to ask. "Where am I? What hospital is this?"

"You're in Vancouver," said the nurse. "In the Vancouver General intensive care. You've broken your back in a car accident and you might not be able to move for a bit. So just rest. Don't try to move."

And having dropped that bombshell, she left, leaving Willy furious, scared, and desperately trying to move something besides her head.

Chapter 2

WHEN WILLY HAD FIRST COME home from the hospital, her younger sister Emily stood beside the driveway, not saying anything, while her mom and dad eased Willy out of the car and into the wheelchair. Even though they had been practising at the hospital, they bumped into each other and fussed over the footrests. They placed a blanket over Willy's knees even though it was a mild spring day. They kept asking her if she was okay until she wanted to scream at them.

Instead, Willy said she was tired and wanted to lie down. Her mom and dad fussed some more, getting her out of the wheelchair and into bed. She immediately hated this downstairs bedroom. She wanted to be upstairs in her familiar room, with the photos of horses and her green striped wall-paper and plush carpet. This room had once been her dad's study: wood-panelled walls, dark brown carpet, pictures of flowers. Now, even with the new pink wallpaper, it felt all wrong. Why couldn't her parents at least have moved her pictures downstairs?

She had curled up in the bed and stared out the window. At least she was out of the hospital with its beeping machines, crappy food, nurses coming in at all hours to ask her how she was feeling. Out of rehab with the kindly helpful therapists, and not one of them ever asking her what she was going to actually do with her life.

After a while, she stopped talking to them. Then of course some counsellor came in, acting concerned to get her to talk about her "condition," as they called it.

But while Willy was lying there, her sister Emily had come and stood beside the bed. Emily, with her blonde curly hair and blue eyes, was only eight.

"I missed you," she whispered.

Willy felt tears start in her eyes but instead she only reached out her hand and grabbed Emily's strong small hand in hers.

"I missed you too," Willy said.

"Are you going to walk again?" Willy looked at Emily's wide open blue eyes. She had always been her pet. Willy watched over Emily after school because their mom was at work. She had always been the one who made sure Emily was safe and happy, the one who read her stories and made her after-school snacks. She had helped take care of Emily since she was a baby.

"Yes," said Willy, "I am. No matter what anyone says. Somehow."

"Mom and Dad said you were a paraplee . . ."

"Paraplegic."

"Yeah. But Mom and Dad told me that means you might never walk again?" Emily looked as if she were going to cry. Her face was white with red circles high on her cheekbones.

"No sweetie, I'm not staying this way," Willy whispered fiercely. "I'm going to walk and then I'm going to run and ski and ride horses again. You'll see."

Yet she hadn't got better. At first despite her sullen outward attitude, she had secretly tried to believe in everyone's hopeful encouragement. But the weeks passed and nothing changed.

Every day, Em came in after school and told her about her adventures. She came in smelling of fresh air and school and bubble gum. She told Willy stories about her friends and their quarrels and friendships. Every afternoon, Willy looked forward to her visit. It was a breath of fresh air in her life. Their mom would bring in a snack and was at least smart enough to leave them on their own.

Willy wondered if Emily thought it was embarrassing to have a sister who was crippled. She found the whole thing embarrassing herself. At first, people had said things to her like, "You've got your whole life ahead of you," or, "You can do whatever you want," but they didn't bother explaining what kind of life she was going to have or how she could do what she wanted.

Because, until that other car had slid on the ice through an intersection and bulleted into her side of the car she was riding in, she had been lucky, unafraid and conscious of her own secure place in the world. Bad things happened to other people somewhere else, not to her. Not to her family.

And despite her brave words to Em, she still wasn't any closer to getting out of the wheelchair than she had been when she came home, despite the best efforts of the physio-therapist, the family counsellor and her parents.

Today, Willy sat beside the bedroom window and watched it rain. Up in the mountains it would still be snowing, but the ski hill had just closed for the season. It was April. Spring was coming. Her friends were down at the community centre, at the opening of the brand new swimming pool. No one had mentioned it to her. They didn't have to. It was all over Face-book, her used-to-be friends posting about when and where and who was going. Everyone was going, except her. No one had invited her. It was okay. She didn't care.

Who cares about anything? she thought. Not me. I am nothing, I am no one, I will just sit here and forget about everything, like friends and skiing and swimming and riding.

She was so utterly bored. She had lots of books, plus a new laptop computer. She was sitting in her wheelchair in a pretty pink room in the downstairs bedroom of her family's house, with a new bed and new drapes and a new desk. She hated all of it. Buying her a new computer and new furniture wasn't going to change her state of being a worthless cripple.

Nor was she going back to school, as her parents and the social workers at the rehab centre had been urging her to do. She could see it all too clearly — being picked up by the special bus, with a wheelchair lift and maybe an attendant who would talk to her in a loud, falsely sympathetic voice as if she were deaf and stupid. The attendant would probably call her "dear."

And then arriving at school while her used-to-be friends pretended to be sympathetic and then giggled to each other in the washroom behind her back.

"Willa," called her mom. "It's almost time for your physio. Are you ready to go?" That question meant — had she wheeled herself into the bathroom, hoisted herself out of the wheelchair and onto the toilet and back into the wheelchair? Yes, she had.

At least her arms still worked. But her legs flopped around, helpless, limp, dead things. She hated her legs.

"Yeah," she called back. Physio. More like torture. The physiotherapist pushed and pulled at her legs as if they were made of clay. She went on sitting until her mother came briskly into the room.

"C'mon, darling," she said in that way-too-cheery voice she always used now. "Let's be right on time and hope we don't have to wait too long. There's nothing to read there. Don't forget to bring a book."

When Willy didn't respond, her mom grabbed the handles of the wheelchair and began to turn it. Willy let her feet flop on the floor so the wheelchair wouldn't move.

"I can do it myself," she said.

"Fine," said her mother. "Then do it please, darling. You know we can't be late for physio. They have to stay on time. They have a lot of patients."

Willy waited for the few more minutes that she knew would drive her mother into a fine froth of exasperation before very slowly wheeling herself out of the room, down the hall to the front door, which her mom was holding open, and down the newly built wooden ramp to the door of the van. Her mother hoisted her into the passenger seat and then folded the wheelchair and put it in the back of the van. During the fifteen-minute ride to the clinic, Willy stared out the window and her mom stared at the wet road. It was pouring rain. Willy stared past the rain to the streets of the small town she knew so well, streets she had run down, bicycled down, her favourite stores, her favourite restaurant — the Other Side — which closed in the winter and reopened in the spring. Its reopening was always a cause for celebration in the town.

At the physio clinic, Willy's mother opened the back of the van, got out the wheelchair, lifted Willy down from the passenger seat into the chair, and then Willy wheeled herself into the physiotherapy clinic.

"I'm just going to run to the bookstore, darling," her mother chirped as she was going in the door to the waiting room. "Anything you want?"

Willy resisted the urge to say, "Yeah, a suicide manual."

"Bye, Liz," said the receptionist.

After Willy's mother left, the receptionist came briskly out from behind her desk, grabbed the wheelchair, wheeled it down the hall and left her in the physiotherapy room.

After some more waiting, there was a forty-five-minute session in the strong hands of the physiotherapist. When the physio had finished lifting Willy's legs up and down, bending and pulling them in different directions, with variations on massage and then some other painful twisting manipulations, she helped Willy back into the wheelchair. Then she pulled up a chair and sat beside her. She tried to look sympathetically into Willy's eyes, which Willy evaded by looking at the floor. Willy thought next time she would remember to wear a hoodie so she could pull it over her eyes.

"You know, Willa, getting well isn't just a physical process. It's mental and emotional as well. We're trying to help you. But your attitude is not helpful."

Willy said nothing, staring at the wall, posters of puppies and kittens. Yick. All she wanted to do was go home and sit and watch the rain some more. She felt exhausted. Maybe she would just go to bed, curl up under the covers, and sleep the afternoon away.

"Everyone wants the best for you. Your mom and dad have

done everything they can. Your mom has taken a year off work to look after you. And you need to do your share. Are you doing your exercises at home?"

"Sometimes," Willy said. She stared down at her hands lying in her lap. At least they still worked. She wriggled her fingers. It seemed so easy. Why didn't it work for her toes?

The physio sighed. She was young and blonde and thin. She looked as if she worked out every day. Her name tag read Sandra. Sandra West. The physio. The torture lady. Her parents talked about her as if she could produce miracles. So far, for Willy, she hadn't.

"Your body is still getting over the trauma of the accident. It will take a long time but there is some possibility that you might be able to walk again. But you have to do the work to make that happen."

"Walk how?" Willy snapped. "Walk with a cane? Or two canes? With a walker like a stupid cripple?" She stared at the puppies again.

"That's up to you," Sandra said. "You can't give up. You have to keep trying, working, and you will get your life back. It won't be the same as before but it can still be rewarding. Even in a wheelchair, life can be rewarding." She paused. "Is there anything more I can help you with?"

Willy stared at her. All kinds of words flashed through her mind, more like howled. How could she tell this blonde smiling woman that everything she cared about in her life was now gone, all the things that once made her Willy Cameron.

Sports: skiing and riding and swimming. Friends, laughing, and shopping, new clothes, being young, being pretty. No one seemed to know or care what she had lost. They all seemed to think she should just get on with her life, some-how. What life? She didn't even know who she was anymore, or what she cared about, or why she should bother caring at all.

"I'm fine," she said. She looked at her hands again. Her nailed were ragged, chewed. She hid them under the edge of her shirt.

"Okay, I'll see you next week," Sandra said.

Willy and her pathetic life were dismissed. Sandra wheeled her back down to reception. Her mother wasn't there.

"Your mom will be just a few minutes," the receptionist said. "She phoned. She'll be right here. Not to worry."

Yeah, like she couldn't even sit here for a few minutes by herself. "Whatever," she muttered.

Willy looked around for a place to park herself. A guy was sitting in the chair next to the door, reading a magazine. He looked up and grinned. Dark hair, dark eyes, white teeth, strong shoulders. He looked just a bit older than her. So what was he doing here? He didn't say anything, just went back to his magazine.

"Ben, Sandra will see you now," trilled the receptionist. She was blonde too. Is that all they hired in this office? Her name tag read Katie.

Ben stood up. He had to hold on to the chair arms and

hoist himself up. He walked stiffly and carefully down the hall.

"What's with him?" asked Willy.

"Juvenile arthritis," said Katie. "It's very painful but he's doing well."

Willy stared down the hall where Ben was just meeting Sandra at the door of her office. He looked back, saw her staring, gave her a thumbs up and disappeared into the office.

Chapter 3

"NO," WILLY SAID. "No, no, no."

"But if it would help?" asked her mom.

"I am not going to see a stupid counsellor. I had enough of it in rehab. And look, oh gee, I am still sitting in this chair. So what good did it do?"

"Honey, you need someone to talk to. You have made it plain that you don't want to talk to your father or me."

"You don't talk. All you do is lecture."

Willy and her mother glared at each other. Her father sat helplessly at the other end of the gleaming dining-room table. Her father and mother. Elizabeth and Donald Cameron. Until Willy's accident, the perfect middle-class couple with a perfect middle-class life. Her mom was blonde and wore lovely new outfits to her work as a high school English teacher.

Her dad was good looking. They read books and magazines plus newspapers. They had lots of friends who were just like them. Boring as could be, right down to their names. Plus two lovely children. Named after famous writers — Willa Cather and Emily Bronte. Of course, English teacher geekiness.

Willy's sister Emily was at school because it was the middle of the afternoon. Willy's father had come home from his work as a loans officer at the local Credit Union so they could all "talk."

All her mother did now was stay home with Willy. She cleaned the house and cooked and vacuumed and read books and stayed home all day, except for driving Willy to appointments. At least when she'd been a teacher, she'd had a life. Willy felt as if the accident had wrecked her mother's life along with her own.

Most of the time, Willy sat in her room by herself, played computer games in which she had no interest, read her friends' postings on Facebook and stared out the window. The people she used to hang out with were busy with their own lives. People had phoned when Willy first came home from the hospital but it was so awkward. She didn't want to talk about the accident. She couldn't remember it anyway.

Her school counsellor came and talked to her about going back to school and then, when she said she wasn't ready, the counsellor suggested she look into doing school at home through correspondence. "Just for the time being," said the counsellor, "until you are ready to join our school community again."

Her high school friends had come in twos and threes at first. They asked how she was feeling, and then they went away quickly and didn't come back again. Some friends, Willy thought. So that's what friendship was worth.

Today her father had decided they should all have a family meeting, so they had gathered around the dining-room table.

"Sandra said you had some chance of getting your legs back because there is still some movement in them, but you have to change your attitude, do your exercises, get out more," Willy's mom said. "Instead you sit in your room day after day. Frankly, Willy, we're really worried about you."

"And where should I go, Mommy dear? Should I go watch my friends having fun at the pool? Should I go to the school dances and watch them all make out?"

"Willy, don't be so rude to your mother," her father rumbled helplessly. "You know we all want the best for you. We all want the same thing, for you to get better."

"No, you don't," Willy snapped. "You just want a nice, acceptable, well-behaved daughter who sits around and goes places in her wheelchair and is nice to everyone and never complains. That's not what I want. I want my life back. I want to be who I was. I liked that Willy. She had fun. She had a lot going for her. Is a counsellor going to do that for me, give my life back? No way. She's going to tell me to adjust, come to terms with being a lousy cripple, get on with my life, all that crap. No, I'd rather sit in my room and die of boredom. Which is where I'm going."

She grabbed the wheels of her chair and turned it towards the bedroom.

"Come back here, Willy, don't do this," her mother cried. But Willy wheeled herself into her room and slammed the door with one hand.

A few minutes later, there was a timid knock on the door. It opened and her father's head peeked around it. He came in and pulled a chair away from the desk so they could sit side-by-side staring out the window. Willy suddenly noticed how his belly sagged over the belt of his grey slacks, how his hair was receding and turning grey. He had always been so trim and fit. He went to the gym and worked out. Other girls had told her that her dad was good looking. He always wore a white shirt and a blue tie and a tailored suit to work.

She remembered how, when she was little, he had taught her to shoot a basketball at the park. He used to tell her stories of how he'd been such a star athlete in high school. But they had stopped playing basketball long before her accident. Her dad was always too busy. She turned her head away.

"Willy, what the heck," he said. Willy turned her head to stare. He sounded weird, as if he might cry.

"I don't know how to deal with this," he said. "Loans, money, figures, that I can understand. Feelings, not so much.

But you know, you're my kid. What can I do? I care about you. If I could buy you some legs, I would."

He had tears in his eyes. Willy was shocked. Her dad never cried.

Willy sighed. She wanted to curl up in his lap as she had when she was little but instead she looked out the window. "It's not your fault. It's nobody's fault. That's the problem. If there was someone to be mad at, I would be. But there's no one. The girl who smashed into the car I was in was just another kid. How can I be mad at her? But she's walking around and I'm not."

"Baby, you're fifteen. You've got your life ahead of you. You can still do whatever you want, go to school. Have a career. You're still beautiful. You're still smart."

"Dad, I was a jock, remember. I rode horses. I went skiing. I played basketball. Like you used to."

"Yeah, I know, Willy." He sighed, wriggled in his chair, scratched the back of his head. "Can I do anything at all? I mean, you know, I would do anything."

"Yeah, get Mom off my back. Tell her to leave me alone. Tell her to go back to work. She's making me crazy vacuuming all day."

"What about the counsellor?"

"No. No way."

She stared out the window some more. When she looked around, he was gone. She hadn't heard him leave.

■

"Can we at least go to the library?" her mother asked. "I can't stand sitting around like this."

"I never wanted you to stay here with me."

"You can't be home on your own. It isn't safe. Someone has to be here and that someone is me. As much as you resent it."

"Fine, let's go to the library. Whatever."

If Willy went to the library in the afternoon, no one from her school would be there. And she was out of books. Reading was the one place into which she could escape for long periods. Curled up on her bed with a decent fantasy novel was the closest thing to peace she could find. She would read long into the night until she was finally tired enough to sleep.

At the library, Willy wheeled herself slowly along the rows of books, from the bookshelf of new books, through the juvenile section, past the mysteries, along the rows of novels. The pile of books on her lap grew steadily. Then past the animal section. She hesitated. There was the new book on riding. She had read about it. Why read it? Why torture herself? But in spite of herself, her hand reached out and pulled it off the shelf. She could, at least, look at the pictures. Then she went to the movie section where she grabbed four or five DVDs.

But when she turned to wheel herself away from the movie section to the circulation desk, she froze. There was that guy she had seen at the physiotherapy office. What was his name? Ben. Right. Dark-brown curly hair. Big smile. White teeth. White t-shirt and worn blue jeans.

He looked up and saw her and smiled. "Hey," he said.

"Hey," she replied. No, she didn't want to talk or explain why she was in a wheelchair or why she wasn't in school in the middle of the afternoon. How could she get out of this? And why was he in the library in the middle of the afternoon instead of at school?

"Wow, now that's a pile of books," he said. He grinned and came over to her, peered at her books. "Hey, you're reading those new Tolkien stories. One of my faves. Right on. Oh, and that new training book. It's great. I just finished it. So, do you ride?"

What a stupid question. She shrugged. She didn't want to talk about riding. "Sorry, I have to go. My mom will be waiting."

He actually turned red. "No, I mean, I'm crippled and I still ride. It's cool. It's helped me a lot."

"Yeah, that's nice. Good for you." She turned her wheelchair and pushed herself furiously across the floor. "Whatever," she said under her breath.

"Hey, wait, sorry, that came out all wrong." He hurried to get in front of her and blocked her way. "But I do ride, at the Therapeutic Riding Centre here in town. I do dressage and jumping. It's helped me a lot."

"Well, my goodness," she said. "I'm so happy for you. But I have to go."

She grabbed the wheels of her chair. This time, he stood aside and watched her leave.

But when she was home and curled up in bed, his words stuck in her head. They kept going around and around. They didn't make any sense. Why would he think she could still ride when she was so obviously paralyzed? He had said he still rode horses, at the Therapeutic Riding Centre. He had called himself a cripple. He sure didn't look crippled. What was it the receptionist had said, he had arthritis? Juvenile arthritis. What did that mean?

And why had she been so rude to him when he was obviously just trying to be nice? He would be totally right never to speak to her again. But who wanted to be friends with a depressed cripple anyway?

"You're not crippled. You have a temporary physical limitation," her mother always said whenever Willy referred to herself as crippled. "Your doctor says there is hope. You mustn't forget that."

But Willy used the word "crippled" because it described exactly what she was.

She began to think about riding. She couldn't help it. She missed it so much. The warm smell of horses. The powerful feeling of a horse's body moving underneath her. Soaring over a jump, or cantering through the grass.

She had never had a horse of her own but she used to ride at a local stable. One of the women there had a horse she didn't have enough time to ride, a tall black horse that loved to gallop and jump. Loki. Willy was his regular rider. She had taken him in a number of shows and had always come home with ribbons.

But to ride, she needed strong legs, and strong hands, a good straight back, and needed to be physically fit. She would never ride again. Even if, by some miracle, she could get on a horse, she would never make a fool of herself by attempting to ride, flopping around like a rag doll, unable to do anything properly. Still, she could dream about it. And she had. She did. She remembered dreaming about it while she was still in the hospital, a vivid dream, not just of riding but flying on the horse.

Then she had woken in the morning to a dull green-painted hospital room, the buzzing of fans and machines, various machines beeping, clicking, humming. A world that was even greyer and drearier and more without hope than it had been the day before.

Tonight, even reading didn't work to distract her or let her sleep. But she couldn't get up and sit at her computer without help. She just had to lie in bed. She wanted to look up juvenile arthritis. What if she started screaming and woke everyone up? Her parents would be upset and her little sister would be scared. No, it wasn't worth it.

Eventually she fell asleep and woke to the usual routine. Her mom had to help her in and out of the shower, help her get dressed, wheel her out to breakfast. But soon it was almost noon and she was so bored. Outside, flowers were blooming and bright green leaves were unfurling on the maple trees along the street. She wanted to go outside and just take a walk. She wheeled herself around in circles. She looked out the window. She turned her television on and off, on and off.

Maybe she could look up suicide recipes on the Internet.

And then someone rang the front doorbell. Probably someone exciting like a friend of her mother's. Or the paper-boy, or maybe, oh joy, a counsellor.

But it was none of those. Her mother came to her open bedroom door, smiling too widely, showing far too many teeth in a bright and brittle attempt to be cheerful.

"Look, darling, we have a visitor. Come on out and say hi, and I'll make us some tea."

Willy wheeled around. Through the door, she could see Ben standing in the dining room, by the table, with his head down, staring intently at the carpet. Oh, no. Very slowly, she wheeled her way out of her room.

He watched her coming. She gritted her teeth. She hated it when someone watched her manoeuvring in the wheelchair.

"Hey," he said, as she came closer. "I came to apologize." His face was red.

"For what, exactly? I was the one who was rude."

"For making you feel bad. It came out all wrong somehow."

Willy stared at him. "I just can't talk about riding," she said. "Ever." Then she added, "How did you find me?"

"It's a small town. First, I asked the librarian about you and got your name, and then I looked you up in the phone book. I phoned your mom and told her you had forgotten a library book and asked if it was okay if I came over. I told her we met at physio. So it's a good thing I'm not some psycho."

"Oh." She felt stunned. She was amazed that he had come.

She had been so mean to him at the library. And now he was apologizing. Wrong way around.

"I'm sorry, too," she said. "I was so weirded out at the library. It's just . . . you reminded me, about riding and everything. I'm not really like that. It's just . . ." She gestured at the wheelchair.

Now they were both silent. Willy looked away, out the window to the sunny street. Her mother came in with a teapot, cups and cookies, all piled on a tray and began to assemble them on the table. Willy slumped in her wheelchair.

"Isn't this nice, Willy. So kind of you to come by, Ben." Willy's mother ignored the silence, the fact that Willy and Ben were both staring at the floor, and just kept talking. "Now Ben, is that your name? You must be new in town? I don't remember seeing you around."

"We came this spring," he said, raising his head. "My dad is an RCMP officer. Joe Morris. He gets transferred a lot."

"So do you know Willy from school?"

"No, as I mentioned on the phone, we met the other day at the physiotherapy office. My appointment was right after hers so we had a chance to say hello. I have juvenile rheumatoid arthritis so the physio really helps. We just started talking and then we ran into each other at the library again."

Now that he was talking, he seemed more relaxed. But Willy couldn't think of a single thing to say. Ben and her mother went on talking. Willy stared at the tea that she didn't want, and ate a cookie she didn't want either.

Then her mom said, "Well, I'll leave you guys to have a visit. I've got some things to do."

She left the room. They heard water running in the kitchen.

"So you used to ride?" Ben asked. "Oops, sorry you don't want to talk about it. I forgot."

"It's okay. Yeah, I did. I was good too. Went in a bunch of shows. Jumping. Dressage. Three-day events."

"Wow! Three-day eventing. That's so amazing. And tough. You must really miss it?"

Boy, this guy had a gift for the obvious. "Yes, of course I do, but so what? I miss lots of things. Like having a life."

"I never used to ride at all, but then I got this stupid disease and I could hardly walk. My counsellor thought riding would be good for me. I thought she was crazy but it turned out she was right, for once. It's made a huge difference."

"So what's wrong with you?"

"The arthritis screws up my joints and muscles somehow. It hurts like crap, actually. But riding exercises everything and it helps me keep in shape. And the horses are so cool. I never used to know anything about horses."

"I don't usually feel my legs, although my muscles hurt, especially after that physio lady pounds on them for a while. And after she makes me walk."

"You can walk?"

"Not really. I hold onto those bars and she moves my feet. Even that hurts. It's hard."

"Wow, that's tough. Hey, maybe you should start riding

again. I bet it would help. It really helped me. I didn't believe in it, but after a while, I could feel the difference. Now I walk differently, I stand differently. I think it saved me from being crippled."

"You're crazy. How could I even get on a horse? Or hold on if I got there?"

"No. That's why it's called therapeutic riding. You roll up a ramp in your chair, and then they lift you on the horse. You have people beside you and someone is always leading the horse. And riding the horse exercises all your joints and muscles so your whole body gets stronger. My riding teacher explained it to me. It's called core strength."

"Forget it. I used to know how to ride properly. And now I am going to get led around the arena? Like a pony ride? No thanks. And you're right. I don't want to talk about it."

"But you could really ride after a while. It doesn't have to be like that. There's people who even ride at the Olympic level who are crippled. One woman even rides from a wheelchair. You should at least go have a look. There's videos on YouTube."

"Why should I care? I told you. It's over, that part of my life. Why even think about it?"

"Why not? You could at least try it."

She couldn't answer that question. There were so many answers and none that made any sense. Because it was easier to sit in her room where no one stared at her or asked stupid questions. Because she wanted her old life. Because all she wanted to do was scream and cry; instead she just stared out the window like a stupid zombie.

"I ride after school on Wednesdays at four. Why don't you come by? At least have a look around. Would your mom bring you?"

Willy stared at him. Would the guy never shut up? Finally she shrugged, a little tiny shrug. "Whatever. Yeah, maybe. Probably. She'll do anything if she thinks it'll get me out of the house. She's going crazy with boredom and she won't admit it."

"Would you really come? That would be so cool. And maybe I'll see you at school?"

"No, you won't. I am not going near that place ever again."

"Too bad. Your school is really nice, way better than my last one. My dad was posted up north and the kids were cool but the school was freezing and falling down. It burned down after I left, actually. Good thing. Maybe now they will get a new one. They sure needed one."

They sat still. The silence filled the room. Willy's head was full of questions but she couldn't think of one to ask that would be polite. Finally she said, "You were up north?"

"Yeah, a little town. Sad place. Lots of crappy stuff going on. Drugs, gangs. You know. I was so glad to get out of there."

Silence again. "Guess I'd better go," he said. "Remember, Wednesday at four. Say thanks to your mom for the tea."

He was clearly glad to go. The front door slammed behind him. Willy sat still for a long time. Then she wheeled herself into her room. She wheeled herself to her desk, looked out her window. Memories of riding, along with images of Ben's smiling face intruded on her solitude. She grabbed the edge of the desk, tried hard to pull herself to a standing position. She got halfway and then her legs began to shake and burn and she sat back down. Then she did it again. It hurt as if burning knives were stabbing her muscles. She didn't care. She would never walk. She could see that. She was glad about the pain. It made it clear. It was all lies.

Chapter 4

WILLY HAD MANAGED TO live without thinking too much about the future, about walking again, until Ben had showed up and talked about riding and lit up her hopes again. Hope was an evil monster, she thought, sitting in her room. It was a spider spinning rainbow webs to catch her in. She hated hope. The grey dead place she had been living in was way easier.

Could she really stand to go out in public, be lifted on a horse like a little kid, be led around the ring and then be helped off again? Wouldn't that be worse than nothing? Worse than hoping she'd start to get well. She couldn't decide. She went to sleep, still wondering.

She had seen Ben at physio again this week. They said hello

and smiled. He seemed a bit too glad to see her. But maybe he was bored. Or maybe he was so new in town he still didn't have any friends. He said they had moved here in the spring. Only a couple of months then. He had mentioned his dad but hadn't said anything about his mom.

This week, all during physio, she gritted her teeth and worked at standing up until the pain in her legs was so bad she felt like screaming. She hooked her arms over the parallel bars and concentrated on swinging each leg forward. They didn't really hold her up. She was doing that with her arms.

"Great job," Sandra said when she was done. Too much emphasis on the great, Willy thought. "Wow, you were really working hard. I know it's slow progress but you are getting a little stronger, each week. Determination is so important."

Willy looked at her. "Thanks," she said finally. All she wanted to do was go home and lie down until the burning knife pain went away. When she wheeled herself out to the waiting room, Ben was there.

"Hey," he said. "You want to go somewhere for a snack later? I've got my dad's car."

"You drive?"

"Yeah ... just got my N license. We could go somewhere, get a coffee, or an ice cream? If you want to wait?"

"No. My mom is here to drive me home. Maybe next week." She felt her face turn red. "Sorry, I really have to go." She turned and headed for the elevators as fast as she could push the wheels of her chair.

"Don't forget about Wednesday," he called after her.

Did the guy never quit? Okay, fine, she would show up Wednesday just to shut him up, just to see that it was totally a geek show and no place for her. And maybe to see him again although that was silly to think about. But then she'd make her excuses and go home and she'd never have to see him again. And she was never ever going out for ice cream in this town where she might run into her ex-friends.

Never.

First she had to ask her mom to drive her to the riding centre without her mom getting all excited and hopeful and way too enthusiastic. She mentioned it that night at dinner, trying very hard for casual.

"Ben asked me to come watch him ride," she said.

Her mother paused, a forkful of roast chicken halfway to her mouth. "Oh, that's wonderful, darling. I'm sure he's a very good rider. Which stable is it?"

"It's no big deal. It's Orchard Stables. You know over on the west side. It's not very fancy."

"Orchard Stables? Oh, that's the one where the handicapped kids ride. I read about it in the paper. They say it's very good. I guess they have a regular program as well. Is that where Ben rides?"

"Yeah, but he rides in the handicapped program."

"He does?"

"Yeah, he's crippled, Mommy, just like me."

"He is?"

"Yeah, remember, he has arthritis. The point being, I need a ride to the Orchard Stables at four p.m. on Wednesday. Is that all right?"

"Yes, of course."

"Thanks."

"Are you going to ride, Willy?" This was from Emily.

"No way."

"Why not?"

"Because."

"But you like riding. You were great. Remember when you won that big silver cup thing and they put your picture in the paper?"

"Shut up."

"Why?" asked Emily. "Why won't you go riding? And don't tell me to shut up!"

"Kids." This from Willy's dad. He didn't look up from his plate.

For a moment there was silence.

"Well, why won't you go riding?" Emily asked. "They have a thing there, a ramp thingie for wheelchairs. We saw it on a field trip."

"You went there?"

"Yeah, last year, with the school. They had really nice horses. A couple of them were pretty old though. But they were really friendly."

"What kind of people were there?"

"You mean the teachers? I dunno. They were nice."

"No, the riders, dummy," Willy snapped.

"There was an old lady, I think. And some kids. I didn't really notice. We had to help pick up poop. It was gross." She made a face.

Willy sighed. No way did she want to hang out with old ladies and little kids while they stared and asked questions or whatever. So she would go to be polite and watch Ben and say nice things and then she would come home again and forget the whole thing. And maybe change her physio appointment time so she didn't run into him again.

Wednesday was a bright clear May morning. Willy spent the morning at her computer, catching up on her school correspondence lessons. She worked carefully. It was too easy but she just wanted to get it done so her mom had no excuse to nag. The lessons were made for dummies. She could power through a week's worth in a couple of days. Finally, she emailed them to her tutor and pushed her wheelchair away from her desk. She stared out the window. It had been three months now since her accident and the thing she missed most was the simple act of going outside.

She had always been an active kid. She liked being outside. Hiking, or playing sports, swimming, camping, or just hanging out. Her dad had played on his university basketball team. He had landscaped and organized the backyard behind their house; there was a basketball court in front of the garage, plus a treehouse, a big lawn and a patch for a vegetable garden. She used to spend a lot of time out there.

This morning, the sun splashed it all with light. Robins were on the lawn, sticking their heads down sideways, listening for worms. A jay called from the top of the big maple. She and her dad used to go to the park a lot when she was little, kick a soccer ball, play basketball. But then she had school and he was always busy at the bank.

Willy wheeled over to her mirror. She looked skinny and pale with greasy hair. What a mess she was. She had lost so much weight because she had no appetite. No one ever saw her except her family and caregivers. But today Ben and whoever happened to be at the riding centre would see her.

"Mom," she called. "I'm going to take a shower."

No answer. She hadn't heard her mom go out. No matter. She would do it all by herself. She hated having her mom help her in and out of the shower. She hated having her mom wash her hair and then help her get dressed, picking out clothes that were easy to get on but looked ugly.

She wheeled herself into the big new bathroom she had all to herself. Em had been so jealous. "Why don't I get my own bathroom?" she had whined when Willy first came home.

"Don't talk like that," Willy's mom had answered. "Of course you don't need your own bathroom. And Willy does." But Willy had told Emily they could share it and Emily did. She would come in the morning and use Willy's bathroom to get ready for school. Willy thought Emily was the only person she wasn't mad at. Emily was just a little kid. She still thought life was all flowers and friends and fun. Like I did once, Willy thought to herself.

Willy wheeled into the bathroom, managed, after some struggle, to get her clothes off, all except her underwear. She could take that off in the shower. Then all she had to do was transfer herself sideways from her wheelchair to the seat in the shower, turn the shower on, wash up, and then get herself out. She had done it many times but always with her mother there to help. She hoisted herself out of the chair, onto the shower seat, wriggled out of her panties and turned on the taps. An initial blast of freezing water. Right. Her mom always ran the shower first so it was warm. But then it warmed up. She stretched to reach the shampoo and soap. For the first time since the accident, she revelled in the warm water, the feeling of being clean. When she was done, she turned off the tap and tried to slide herself sideways out of the shower stall and into the wheelchair. But the wheelchair slid sideways as well, and Willy crumpled onto the floor of the shower stall. Her legs and back flashed pain signals, warning signals. She had to get back in the chair. Somehow.

For a moment, she lay there. "Mom," she called. "Mom." Still no answer. Where had her mother gone? Well, fine, she'd just have to figure something out. Still lying down, she managed to wriggle and inch her way slowly backwards until she was out of the shower stall and lying on the linoleum floor. She rolled over until she was beside the wheelchair. Every roll made her back feel as if it were on fire.

Then she inched herself backwards as far as the bed, pulling the wheelchair with one hand. Lying on her side, she reached up, grabbed the mattress with one hand and then the other, and dragged herself up until finally she was sitting on the bed. Exhausted, she lay back and looked at her stupid wheelchair. If only it were a dog and she could call it when she needed to. She lay flat on the bed until her back pain subsided, then she wriggled her way back to the side of the bed and into the wheelchair. Now all she had to do was get dressed.

"Willy," her mom exclaimed from the doorway. "Are you okay? Why are you undressed?"

"I had a shower," she said. "And I was just going to get dressed. By myself," she added.

It had taken her a while to decide what to wear so it was just after four p.m. when Willy's mother turned the van into the driveway of the Orchard Stables. It didn't look impressive, pens outside with horses standing in them, a covered riding arena and a barn attached to it. Willy's mother parked by the barn and then got Willy into the wheelchair. The parking lot wasn't paved but there was a grassy path downhill to the barn. It was bumpy and slow-going, being wheeled in the chair over the grass and rutted dirt full of hoof prints.

Finally, Willy and her mother went up a ramp and through the open door of the barn at one end of the arena. Inside the riding ring were a horse and rider going around beside the high white-painted metal railing, and a red-headed woman who stood in the middle of the ring. There were several white plastic chairs just outside the high metal fence and a couple of people sat and watched.

Then she realized it was Ben who was riding the horse,

guiding it through circles, trotting and cantering. Willy was impressed. She had expected him to be walking around the ring, slowly, on some ancient horse. But this horse was a tall chestnut. It moved with a lot of energy and snap. Obviously not old and tired. The instructor was calling instructions and comments. While Willy watched, Ben stopped in the middle of the ring and after a long conversation with the instructor, slid off and then led the horse from the ring.

Willy's mom pushed her wheelchair down the concrete laneway inside the barn to where Ben and the red-haired woman were now unsaddling the beautiful brown horse, which was cross-tied between two posts.

Willy slowly wheeled up beside them. Even though she was used to horses, she had never been around a horse in a wheelchair. It made her nervous. The horse seemed very large beside her. Willy's mother stood back, away from the horse.

"Willy," Ben said with a big grin. "You came. Yay, we're practising for our first real dressage test at the end of the month. Hey, come around here. This is my teacher, Victoria, and this is her horse, Kit. She's letting me borrow her. Victoria, this is my friend Willy. She used to ride before her accident. But I told her you could get anyone on a horse."

"That was some pretty good riding," Willy said. I'm not getting on a horse again, she thought to herself. Never, ever.

"Ben is one of our best riders. You can pet Kit," Victoria said briskly. "She's used to wheelchairs. Pretty bombproof, this one. We have to make sure our horses are used to every-thing that might happen around them. We have people with all sorts of disabilities who ride here."

Willy scratched Kit's soft shoulder and neck. Kit sniffed the wheelchair and snorted.

"Yes, Ben's riding is really coming along. He's a star around here." She grinned at Ben who ducked his head in embarrass-ment.

Victoria was short and lean with curly red hair. She seemed to radiate energy. "So, you used to ride. Great idea to start it again. The sooner the better. You need to get those muscles working again. Riding will exercise all your muscles and joints and build that important core strength."

"I can't . . ." Willy began. "I don't . . ."

"Can you stand up?"

"Yes, a bit. But only with bars, at the physio."

"Hmm, shouldn't be too much of a problem then. We can run the wheelchair up the ramp, lift you into the saddle. We'll have to see how you do, of course. You would have three walkers, one on either side, so you would be very safe."

"But . . ."

"And we need a form from your doctor. And your parents. Where did I put those? Oh yeah. Just a sec." Victoria went down the hall, rummaged around on a crowded table in the corridor. It held bits of tack, a box of doughnuts, a riding helmet and a clipboard with papers.

She held out one piece of paper to Willy and another to

her mom. "Here's some information on the program, and what we do here. We'll have to find a slot for you, and the right horse." She picked up the clipboard and flipped through its pages. "You'll need to talk it over together when you get home. It's a bit late in our term but you could start next week, right after Ben here. That suit you? Hmm, I would have to put you on Kuna. He's available."

"But . . ." Willy started again and then she stopped. Kit had her head on her shoulder and was gently nibbling her hair. Willy rubbed Kit's soft nose and Kit dropped her head so it was level with Willy's chest. Willy scratched her ears. Kit gave a huge sigh and blew horsey breath all over her.

"Wow, she really likes you," Ben laughed.

"I guess I could try it once . . ." she heard herself saying. The words seemed to come out of her mouth involuntarily.

"Good girl," Victoria beamed. "Now, want a tour? Ben, why don't you come along. You know everyone. You can introduce Willy to the horses."

Victoria grabbed the back of the wheelchair and began pushing Willy along the row of box stalls. Ben and Willy's mom followed. Curious black and brown and golden heads reached out, sniffed at their hands, looked for treats.

"Most of our horses are donated," Victoria said. "But they have great personalities and they really seem to care about what they are doing. I've seen some miracles here with these horses and their riders. Hey, babies. How's my sweet things?"

She had a pocketful of horse cookies and doled them out.

About halfway along the corridor, two women were standing beside a grey horse. "This is Elizabeth," said Victoria, "one of our coaches, and Sharlene, one of our assistants. We have a lot of volunteers as well. Place runs on volunteers, actually. The horses are in the stalls during the day and out in the pasture in the afternoon for a break when they are done riding. That is a lot of work, just getting everyone in and out when they are needed."

Sharlene was young and blonde and Elizabeth was older, with grey hair tied up in a bun. They had the horse tied to a set of posts and were looking at his legs.

"Oh, Blue, how're ya doing, big boy? What's wrong? That darned tendon again?" Victoria asked. "Ben, maybe you can continue the tour. I need to talk to these guys about Blue . . ." All three of them bent over the horse's leg.

"Willy, I'll wait for you in the van," Willy's mom said. She turned and marched down the corridor.

Ben pushed the wheelchair to the end of the corridor and then turned around, introducing each of the horses by name. There were ten horses in the barn. "That's about it," he said cheerfully. "What do you think?"

"It's pretty small," she said.

"Yeah, but the teachers are great. Victoria is amazing, really patient and careful and so is Elizabeth. They both make sure everybody feels safe and then they make sure everyone has a great time. Victoria is such a good teacher. She tells me I will learn one new thing at every lesson. And I do. Plus the horses here love their jobs."

"I used to ride over at Riverview. I leased a horse from a

woman there. A big thoroughbred. It loved to jump. So did I."

"Not too much jumping around here. I'm mostly practising dressage. Getting ready to do a test in June."

"A dressage test? In a show?"

"No, I compete in the national therapeutic riding competition. They video the dressage test here, and then send it in. You have to get classified and then you compete against riders on your own level."

"Really?"

"Yeah, you compete against riders with similar disabilities. I got a first last year."

"Oh."

Couldn't really be much of a competition, she thought to herself. Riding against other cripples.

"So are you really going to come ride here?" Ben asked.

"I'm going for one ride," she said. "I'll see what that feels like. I doubt if it will work though. I don't think I can ride with these." She waved at her legs.

"Oh. Right. But it is great that you are giving it a try."

She already regretted saying yes. "One try," she snapped. "Then we can all forget about it."

Why did she keep doing that, snapping in anger? But she didn't know how to apologize. She knew if she said anything more to Ben about riding, she would start crying and she wasn't about to do that. Oh, how she had missed riding and the smells and sounds of horses, the soft feel of their noses. All this place did was remind her of what she had lost. She was never coming back here. Her mother was waiting for her outside.

Ben pushed her to the open barn door and her mother met them there.

"Let's go," Willy said to her mother, who was smiling, had her mouth open, ready to ask cheerful questions or make a statement about how wonderful it all was. And that was the last thing Willy wanted to hear right now.

"See you soon," Victoria called from down the corridor, where she was still looking at Blue's leg.

Her mother wheeled her across the parking lot and then got her into the van while Ben stood in the barn door watching.

"If you want to talk about it or ask questions, just text me, or give me a call or Facebook me," he called. "That would be great. I really love this place. It would be fun to have someone to share it with."

"Yeah, whatever." She bent her head forward so her long blonde hair swung forward and hid her face. And then her mother got in, started the van, and swung it around in a wide circle, the tires crunching over the gravel driveway. Willy could see Ben standing there looking utterly forlorn. She would have found it almost comical if she hadn't been so angry at herself for being so rude. It was as if a huge bubble of bitter words roiled up from inside her and spilled out of her mouth before she could stop them.

Willy kept her head turned, looking out the window,

despite her mother's attempts to make conversation. At home, she fled as fast as she could push the wheelchair, into the safety of her room, and slammed the door shut. She manoeuvred the wheelchair next to the bed, got herself in and under a quilt and lay there, too mad at herself and the world to do anything else.

"Hey Willy," it was Emily, home from her friend's house, smelling of fresh air, green leaves and mown grass. She didn't knock, just shoved open the door, sat on the bed and bounced a few times, "Hey, guess what. I got an A in English. Mom is soooo happy."

"That's nice," Willy said, poking her head out from the covers, "now go away. I don't feel like talking."

"But Mom said you went to that riding place. She said it's soooo great and you're gonna ride there and everything. And she said this Ben guy is soooo nice. She thinks he really, really likes you."

"Em, please shut up. I live in a wheelchair. I don't have boyfriends. And I look like crap, my hair needs cutting and I'm too skinny. And I'm not going riding."

"So get a haircut, dopey."

Emily bounced on the bed again and ran out of room. Willy's mom was calling, "Dinner, girls. Willy, are you coming?"

Chapter 5

THE NEXT WEDNESDAY, Willy stared out the window at the amazingly bright sunny day. She wished it were raining, foggy, snowing. Anything but sunny and cheerful and bright. She had no excuses not to go riding.

The problem was, she knew if she looked deep into her heart, that she really wanted to go. She missed riding. She missed being around horses. Seeing them. Doing something with them.

And then there was Ben and his wounded forlorn smile as he had watched her leave. She would probably keep seeing him at physio or around town no matter how much she tried to avoid it. It was that kind of small town. She needed to figure out how to stop overreacting. Just be normal around him. Say hello. Be cool yet distant. Wounded yet brave. Keep her real self undercover. But before that, she was going to have to apologize, yet again. Maybe cool and distant was too hard to do. She could just resign herself to being rude and nasty.

She looked at the pamphlet Victoria had pushed into her hand. Significant emotional and physical benefit. Blah blah. Right. Whatever that meant. Sounded like more counsellor speak.

Well, she would try going. Once. Nothing to lose. She didn't have to keep going. If she hated it, she could just go back to sitting in her room.

And if she didn't at least try it, her mom would look wounded and would vacuum the house twice as much. Emily would think she was a chicken but she wouldn't say so. She'd just stop looking up to her older sister and go find someone else to talk to. And her father might decide to never come home, and just live at the bank.

"Willy, you're here," Ben said. His face lit up. "I didn't think you were coming."

She shrugged. This morning, she had made her mother find her riding breeches, boots and helmet. She had looked at them, and slowly, carefully, put on the breeches and boots. Then she had put on a clean white t-shirt and pulled her hair back into a ponytail. Her stomach was in knots. The more she thought about it, the more nervous she became. How could she ride a horse when her legs didn't work? What if she fell off? Yes, there would be people there to catch her but what if the horse got upset by having some crippled person trying to ride him?

He laughed. "I'm going to stick around to watch you. My lesson is done."

She sighed. "Whatever."

Her mom said, "I'll be back in an hour. Are you sure you'll be okay? Are you going to be warm enough? Should I get your coat?"

Willy shot her a look that would have felled a charging grizzly, and her mom's mouth closed. "Okay, see you all later," she said and fled to the van.

"Okay, Willy, let's have a chat," Victoria said, coming out of a stall where she had been saddling a horse. "Ben, buzz off for a bit. Willy come here and relax for a moment. Here are some forms you need to fill out and these you need to have signed by your doctor and your physio."

Willy nodded, as Victoria pulled up a white plastic chair and sat beside her.

Victoria looked at Willy. "So what did happen to you?"

"It was a stupid car accident," Willy said. "I was with a bunch of friends. We were on our way to go skiing. Some teenager driving, going like a bullet, hit the side where I was sitting. I didn't even see her. I didn't know anything until I woke up in the hospital. Everyone else was okay."

"Okay, I understand you've been going to physio for a while? How much movement is there in your legs?"

"Some ..." She hesitated. "I can stand up but I have to

hold on with my arms. I can even walk a little when the physio moves my legs. The doctor said I might be able to walk some day but we'd have to wait. It's been almost six months, and I still can't walk on my own. I don't see how I can ride with no legs."

"But that's great that you have both movement and feeling. Good. Those are very important indicators that there is still nerve function. Now, how much riding have you done?"

"I was Junior High point rider last year at the Kettle Valley show."

"Well done. So you probably have good hands, a good independent seat. You're right, the hard part will be your legs. But we can deal with that. We can use Velcro straps to hold your legs in place and ties to hold the stirrups to the girth. Your legs won't be strong at first but they'll start to improve. Riding exercises all your muscles. How is your sense of balance?"

"Um . . . I don't know. I get dizzy sometimes when I try to stand up."

"Well, that is pretty normal. We'll just watch you and make sure someone is always beside you on both sides. Okay then, let's get started. The sooner the better. I've put you on Kuna. He's an Appaloosa, bit of a hot head at times but very kind and careful with his riders. He's got attitude but you can totally trust him. Let's see. Nice riding boots. Good. Now remember, you'll have people beside you for your whole ride so you can't fall off. Are you nervous?"

"Yes."

"Well, that's normal. But I think after you ride, you will see how safe it is. This is a therapeutic riding centre so we have to make sure that safety is a priority. Safety first, and then we can all have a joyful experience, horses and riders. Okay?"

Willy nodded.

"Okay, Ben, you can come back now."

Ben came back and stood beside Victoria looking anxious and attentive.

"Ben, can you bring Kuna out and help Elizabeth groom and saddle him? Then take him out for a warm-up walk after he's saddled," Victoria said. "I'll get Willy up to the ramp. Sharlene," she called, "can you come and be a side walker? And we'd better have Elizabeth, too, after we get in the ring. Thanks."

Now three people, all wearing riding breeches and paddock boots, were looking at her.

"Okay, here he comes. Willy, come and meet Kuna," Victoria said, pushing Willy to the middle of the row of stalls where there was a tie-up area, with cross-ties for the horses, racks by each stall for saddles and bridles, plus a sink, shelves and an entry gate into the arena. "Kuna, here's your new rider."

Kuna was a dappled brown and white Appaloosa, not too tall but well muscled. Ben snapped his ropes into the cross-tie clips while Kuna nosed Willy's hand, looking for treats, and then nibbled at her hair with his soft lips. Willy tentatively scratched at his shoulder.

Elizabeth brought out Kuna's saddle and bridle, put them

on, checked and double-checked everything while Ben held him still.

"Okay, let's get your riding helmet on and then, as soon as Ben is ready, we'll get you on," Victoria said.

Willy's heart turned over in her chest. Was she ready for this?

After Willy put her helmet on, Victoria pushed the wheelchair up a low sloping ramp at the end of the row of stalls. "Okay, here come your helpers and your horse," she said cheerfully. She positioned the wheelchair carefully on the level deck at the top of the ramp while Ben led Kuna alongside the ramp. Then with Elizabeth on one side, Sharlene on the other and Victoria behind, holding her under her arms, Willy stood up. Victoria helped her swing her leg over the saddle and then Sharlene and Elizabeth steadied her.

"Okay?" Victoria said. "Stirrups might need shortening. Hold on. Must check the girth. And today we'll strap your legs to the stirrup leathers. Is that okay?" She fussed over the tack, then said, "Okay, looks good. Let's go then. Willy, here are the reins. Do you want to hold them? Yes? Okay then. Ben, can you please open the gate."

Willy was shaking. It was all so strange. And amazing. She had to get herself under control. She tried to sit up straight. She tried to push her legs into the stirrups but her legs had no strength or control. How could she ride? What if she just fell over? But Elizabeth and Sharlene were on either side of her. Her legs were strapped into the stirrups, and the stirrups were strapped to the girth. That felt strange as well. She was used to riding with her legs under her own control.

Ben swung open the steel gate, and they all moved into the arena and began walking down the long side of the ring. Willy straightened her back.

To be on a horse again felt good. It had once been her favourite place to be. She had first fallen in love with horses when she was six, at her grandmother's farm. Her grandmother boarded horses, lots of horses, and Willy spent most of the summers with her grandmother. She played with the horses, helped her grandmother take care of them, and was allowed to ride the gentler horses all by herself. When she came back to the town, she asked for, and got, riding lessons. She begged and begged her parents to buy her a horse of her own but they pointed out, far too reasonably, that it cost too much and she had no place to keep it. Eventually, they consented to her leasing a horse and she had found a great horse on which to compete. It had been the perfect arrangement — until Willy got hurt.

Willy tried again to push her legs down as hard as she could into the stirrups but she couldn't really tell where her legs were or what they were doing. Despite how familiar it all felt, she was terrified of falling off. The ground seemed far away. The horse rocked from side to side. Willy lurched sideways and then backwards. "Relax," she told herself. She closed her eyes and then opened them again.

"And whoa," said Victoria. The horse stopped and Willy lurched forward, then sat up straight again.

"How are you doing, Willy. Okay?" Victoria asked. "Tell us

if you aren't okay and we'll stop right away. Are you dizzy?"

"It's okay, I'm fine." She wasn't fine at all. Should she even be doing this? What if she fell off? She was lurching around like a rag doll. It was so embarrassing. But they'd catch her if she fell, wouldn't they?

Victoria fussed again with the stirrups and the cinch and then they started walking again. This time, Willy relaxed more into the motion of the horse. The sense of familiarity came back. She knew how to do this. But her legs were worse than useless. They dangled at Kuna's side like flaps. The group crossed the arena several times, and went around in a couple of wide circles. They stopped and started off again. By the time the lesson was over, Willy's legs and shoulders were aching.

They stopped again in the middle of the ring.

Victoria looked up at her. "Okay, how are you feeling?"

"Good," Willy said.

"Not sore, not too tired?"

"I'm fine."

"Then tell your horse what a good job he did."

Willy was embarrassed. Of course. All good riders praised their horses at the end of a ride. "Good boy, Kuna, you were great. Thanks." She leaned forward, patted the horse's neck, stroked his silky mane.

"Great. Off you go then," Victoria said. "You seemed pretty secure up there. You're a very capable rider. Maybe next week we can do some exercises at a walk and start building your strength. Would that be okay with you?"

Exercises. More exercises. What she wanted to do was gallop around the ring, jumping fences. She wanted to take her horse and go for a long ramble along the trails down by the river. She wanted to feel the coiled pride and strength and response of her horse as they went through a dressage test or jumped big fences.

"Sure," she said.

After they led Kuna back to the ramp, they carefully lifted her off the horse and back into her wheelchair. She settled into the now familiar chair seat. She put her shoulders back. But her body felt different somehow as if something inside her that had been asleep was now awake.

Her leg muscles cramped and ached. She took a deep breath and straightened her back. "I can ride," she said under her breath. But could she? Was this true? She thought about how she had felt on Kuna. She had felt a connection, the same connection she used to have with the horses when she was a little kid, when she rode bareback on her grandmother's farm, with no fear at all. The same connection she had felt when she and Loki were galloping headlong towards a jump and she knew, without a doubt, that he could jump it and they would be fine. How had she known that? She had never questioned herself before.

But the connection was there. It was like electricity. She felt it. She just knew.

Ben pushed her down the ramp. Her mother hadn't appeared yet. Victoria had led Kuna into the corridor, tied him, and was taking the saddle and bridle off, then giving him a brush and cleaning his feet. Ben pushed Willy over beside him.

Kuna bent his head down and nosed her hair. "Oops, you're gonna have horsey slime in your hair," Ben said.

"I don't care," Willy said. She fondled Kuna's soft nose and ears. "I like horsey slime."

"Kuna loves his job here," Victoria said. "These horses are amazing. They seem to really understand what they are doing. He responded to you. You sit well. I think you are going to have a great time here. You must have been a terrific rider before your accident. You're very capable." She bent back down to brush his leg.

"Hey, your mom is here," Ben said. "Want me to take you to the van?"

"No, I'll do it myself." She hesitated. "Um, thanks Ben, it was great. I'll see you next week, okay?" She gave him a big goofy smile. She couldn't help herself. He smiled back, a smile that lit up his whole face.

As she turned the chair and wheeled herself away, she tried to analyze what she was feeling. It was strangely familiar, an echo of her past life. "Capable," she said out loud.

"What did you say?" asked her mom, who met her at the barn door.

"Nothing," said Willy.

That night, Willy lay in the dark on her bed and wiggled her big toe. It barely moved but it was still a fascinating piece of her body, not beautiful, just amazing. The fact that it moved at all meant that she might walk again. That is what her doctor had told her in her last visit there.

"You're young and fit and your body is still adapting," he had said. "If you get any movement at all, it's a good sign. It means it should start to come back gradually. Maybe. We don't ever know for sure. Everybody heals differently."

She remembered lying in the hospital after the accident, after she woke up, staring at her legs, willing them to move. And then, after that, her fury at them and herself when she couldn't walk. She hated the exercises in the swimming pool at the rehabilitation centre when her legs seemed to float off in various directions, toppling her over while the attendant there had to hold her upright. Or she had to hold on tight to the edge of the pool like some kind of helpless clown while her legs floated out behind her like two ridiculous balloons that had been tied onto the rest of her.

Or holding herself up on the parallel bars while the physiotherapist moved her legs for her so they could both pretend she was walking. "Capable," she said to her toe. "You are capable of moving. You move well. Come on, stupid leg. Time to get capable."

Chapter 6

BEN WAS WAITING FOR HER after her next-morning physio appointment. "I told your mom I'd bring you home. There's a great new lunch place in town. Let's go."

"No! I don't go out," she said.

"Why not? It's not a date, it's lunch. Food, you know . . . in this case, it's this funny little French café called Retro Café, real homemade food but if you don't like it, we can go somewhere else."

"No, it's not that." She paused, trying to figure out what to say without sounding like an idiot. "It's just, I don't want anyone to see me, you know, in this thing."

"It's just a wheelchair. The restaurant is easy to get into. I checked it out."

"What if someone from my school is there?"

"Well, what if they are?"

"No. Just take me home," she snapped.

"What do you mean, no?" He had his sad hurt face on again.

"Well, no means no, that's what I heard."

"Look, at least come as far as the restaurant. If there's no one there, then let's just have lunch. I'm starving." He grabbed the handles of the wheelchair and swivelled it towards the door. "Bye, Katie, see you next week."

"Bye, you two. Have fun."

All the way down the hall, into the elevator, out onto the main floor, Willy was ready to burst with fury. Her mother had obviously manipulated this whole situation and put Ben up to taking her out. She could just hear her mother's voice. "She needs some friends. She needs to get out of the house."

But then somehow, they were beside Ben's car and the door was open and he had scooped her up with his strong capable arms, plunked her in the passenger seat, folded her wheelchair, put it in the trunk, and climbed into the driver's seat and she still hadn't said anything.

"I thought you were crippled with arthritis."

"I am," he said cheerfully. "It hurts a bit to shove you around but it was worth it. I told you, the riding has made such a difference."

She turned to look at him but he wasn't looking at her. He was concentrating on getting the car started, and then carefully manoeuvring it out of the parking lot.

Willy sighed. "I haven't been out anywhere since the accident."

"And that was what ... six months ago? Wow, sounds crappy."

"Yeah, something like that."

"No wonder you're so pale," he said. "You need some sunshine. After lunch, do you want to go to the park by the river? I really like it there."

Lunch out and then a walk in the park, Willy thought. It didn't seem like much. Not a big deal. But for some reason she was terrified. She took deep breaths. People did this every day. You went in, sat down, ordered, ate food. Tried not to spill anything. Smiled. Made conversation.

Ben pulled the car into the restaurant parking lot, stood up, lifted out the wheelchair and set it up, then hoisted her out of the passenger seat and put her into the chair. His arms felt warm and strong. Willy knew her face was red.

Ben pushed her towards the door.

"Ben," she said.

"What?"

"It's ..."

He stopped the wheelchair, came around, knelt in front of her, looked at her. His brown eyes had flecks of gold and green in them, he was wearing a brand new black hoodie, his brown-black hair looked as if he had just had it cut.

"It's just lunch," he said. "No pressure. But I'll make a deal with you. We'll come back here, next year at this time, and you can walk in the door. Okay? This year, I'm buying. Next year, your turn."

It was too much. Too good. She took a deep breath. "Deal," she said.

He pushed her in the door. He was right. It was easy to get inside. There was a wheelchair ramp, a door that opened automatically. Inside it was dim light, a wooden floor. A nice-looking man smiled, led them to a table and left them menus. Ben tucked the wheelchair under the table and Willy looked around. No one she knew. A table of men by the window. A couple of women having lunch together.

"How're you doing?" he asked. He grinned at her. "Nice place, eh? The food is great. My dad says the owners are from France. They moved here to get out of the city smog and have time to go bicycling."

"Yes, it's nice," Willy said. There were wall hangings and carvings. A shelf full of antiques. Even some books. The man came back and they ordered food — or rather, Ben ordered the food. He seemed so knowledgeable about everything. Poutine and hamburgers and milkshakes.

"We used to live in Vancouver for a while when I was younger. Before we went up north." Ben grinned. "We ate out a lot. My dad's a terrible cook. Now we come here when we want real food. In Vancouver, there seemed to be a Thai or a Vietnamese restaurant on every corner so that's what we ate. Up north, we ate caribou or seal. Yuck!"

"Why did you move here?"

"My dad was transferred. You know, they move cops all over the place. We never stay anywhere for long."

"What's that like, having a cop for a dad?"

"It's okay, although there's always some dude in school who wants to smoke dope or do drugs in front of me to see what I'll do. I really don't care."

"What's your dad like?"

"Just, you know . . . like a dad. What about your parents?"

"I have the world's most ordinary boring family. Dad's a banker, Mom's an English teacher. Or she was. Before my accident. All they do these days is worry about me. Makes me crazy so I just don't talk to them."

"Who do you talk to?"

"No one. My little sister Emily, sometimes. My best friend Lailla, but I haven't talked to her for a long time. She's got school and stuff. She's probably found some new friends."

"Wow, that's rough. I thought after an accident, you'd have a counsellor or some support group thing."

"I went to a counsellor once. She wanted me to adjust to my condition. After that I wouldn't talk to her. She told my mom I had anger issues, and maybe I needed drugs to calm me down. She said I might have post-traumatic stress or something."

"So, do you have anger issues?"

"Damn straight."

They both laughed. Their food came. The food was fantastic and Willy ate more than she usually ate for lunch. She realized how long it had been since she enjoyed such a simple thing as eating. Ben told her silly dumb blonde jokes and she laughed. She hadn't laughed for a long time either.

After lunch, Ben loaded her and the wheelchair back in the car, got in and drove her to the park on the outside of town near Victoria's stables. It was an old park, a neglected sort of place, huge trees, a path that ran beside a river. A few picnic tables. Ben drove to a spot overlooking the river, and this time they wandered along the paved path that ran by the river, Ben pushing the wheelchair, until they came to a big log where Ben could sit.

They sat and watched the sun sparkle on the river. The light was hot on Willy's face and arms. She hadn't been so warm for a long time. It was on the edge of uncomfortable but she didn't care.

Tiny green curled sparks of leaves were unfolding on the maple trees above the path. Mallard ducks bobbed and ducked in the reeds beside the river. They didn't talk much. After a while, Willy said, "I should go home. My mother will be worried. She doesn't even know I'm here."

"Does she worry a lot?"

"All the time. Non-stop. It's her middle name. She changed so much after the accident, it was like it broke something in her too."

Ben laughed. "My dad never worries about me. Some days I think he forgets I'm even here. See down there, past those trees. There's a path and a kind of hidden spot in the brush there among the rocks. It's like a cave. I spend a lot of time there, just hanging out. Someday when you can walk, I'll take you down there."

"What about your mom?"

His face changed. "She's dead," he said. "Come on, I'll take you home."

That night, Willy wiggled her toe some more, and then, ever so slightly, she moved her foot. She wanted to jump out of bed and yell out the window but she only lay there and remembered the day, the sun on the new leaves, the smell of the river, Ben smiling at her as he lifted her into the car.

Chapter 7

SHE WENT RIDING ONLY once a week. In addition, she had school classes online, plus physio, and visits to the library. The days started to zip by a little faster, in sharp contrast to the boring dull days after her accident. She and Ben had gone for coffee a couple of more times. After the lunch out, he had seemed to pull back a bit. She couldn't quite figure it out.

One day, several weeks after she had begun at the riding centre, Victoria said briskly, "Okay, today is a test. I am going to let you try riding by yourself. As far as I can tell, you don't need someone to lead you around; you're quite secure on a horse. But we'll keep your legs strapped down. Elizabeth will be standing by with us in the ring if you need help."

"Really?" Willy was so surprised that her voice squeaked.

"Is that too frightening?"

Willy thought about it. "No, it's not. I feel fine riding. It was scary at first but now it's okay."

"Great. Kuna is definitely responding to you. You are able to ride him well just with your back and your seat bones and your hands. I know you don't really have your legs back yet but we'll see how it goes, okay?"

Victoria led Kuna into the ring, then checked Willy's girth and stood back. "Okay, signal him to move on." Willy tried to put pressure on Kuna's ribs with her legs but nothing happened.

"I can't," she said. "I can't do it. My legs won't move. I can't ride him."

"That's okay," Victoria said. "Just sit there for a minute. I've got an idea."

She left the ring and then came back with two long dressage whips. "Okay," she said. "This might be awkward at first but I want you to use one on either side, as a substitute for your legs. Kuna will have to learn this too. Just tap him very gently, both sides, as a signal to move on. I'll tell him to move at the same time. Can you manage?"

The whips felt awkward in her hands. Reins, whips, a lot to manage.

"When your legs are stronger," Victoria said, "you won't need the whips. They are just to signal the horse, so be careful. Just little taps, a little bit of pressure. Understand?"

Willy nodded, her lips pressed together firmly.

Victoria said, "Now, walk on."

Willy tapped Kuna just behind her legs with both whips, and obediently, he moved forward. She lurched backwards. She had gotten too used to other people telling him to move.

"Good," said Victoria. "Now tell him 'whoa.' Gentle pressure with your bum and your hands." Willy tried and miraculously, Kuna obeyed.

"Ready?" Victoria asked. "Try it again, little taps. Kuna, walk on."

This time when he moved forward, she was ready. They went around the ring twice, stopping and starting and then did it again in the other direction.

When Willy slid off and was helped into her wheelchair, she felt exhausted but triumphant. It wasn't much. It wasn't galloping over fences. But she had done it, all by herself, done something, as Victoria said, "capable."

The next day was physio.

"How are you, Willy?" asked Sandra cheerfully. She was always cheerful. At the beginning of her treatment, Willy had tried to think of various smart-ass responses to that question. Everyone asked it. Doctors, nurses, everyone in rehab. She had no answer. "I'm crippled and pissed off about it," she usually thought but didn't say. Normally, she just didn't answer. But today she said, "I'm getting better."

Sandra started to nod cheerfully then stopped. "You are?" she asked.

"Yes," said Willy. "Yesterday I rode at the Therapeutic Riding Centre and my legs moved. Not much but a little. I couldn't see it but I could feel it."

"Wow, that is good news. It means you are getting stronger and your muscles are starting to respond. The brain and the nervous system are amazing. Your brain is making new paths and your nerves are healing. This is very exciting. So let's see what is going on in your muscles."

Carefully, Sandra went all over her muscles, asking Willy to push or pull or hold against the pressure she was exerting with her hands. When she was finished, she stood back. "Yes, definitely what we call flickers of movement. Hard to say exactly how far you will progress but it's exciting. It's like the nerves in your muscles are waking up. It's a slow process, Willy, and we never know how far it will go."

"I'm going to walk," Willy said. "And I'm going to ride." Her voice was loud and she didn't care. She was so sick of health people and how careful with words they all were.

"Well, we'll see," Sandra said carefully. She added "Now, let's move on and see what we can do to support and facilitate your progress."

Willy could now stand for longer periods of time, still with help, and holding on to the parallel bars. Usually, Sandra picked up her foot and slowly moved it forward. One foot at a time, supporting herself with her arms, Willy would move. But today, when Sandra picked up her foot, Willy felt the muscles in her calf tighten. It wasn't much. It wasn't even visible but it was more than she had felt since the accident.

"It moved!" she said to Sandra. "My leg, it moved. I felt it."

"I didn't see anything."

"It was inside. I felt it. I really did!"

"That's good, Willy." Sandra felt along her leg. "Yes, definitely muscle is building there. New muscle. It's responding. Let's keep going."

At the end of the session, Willy collapsed into her wheelchair, exhausted. "Walking is hard work," she said.

"Yes, it's amazingly complicated. Takes your whole body just to lift one foot." Sandra laughed. "Really, you lift your foot with the top of your head. The muscles link all the way down."

"That's so weird," Willy said. "I never thought about that before."

That night at home, she ate dinner, laughed over some school gossip with her sister, and then wheeled into her room and did her schoolwork.

Later that night, when the house was silent, sitting on the side of the bed, holding on to the back of her wheelchair, she tried and tried again to lift one foot and put it down again. She could feel the muscles in her calf flex and expand. Finally she was able to lift up her heel.

I need to get fit, she thought. She flopped over onto her back. All this sitting around in a wheelchair had meant her muscles weren't being used. Her brain wasn't being used. She had become such a boring person. She had wanted her life to fall apart, to be boring. She had been so angry. When had she stopped being angry? Actually, she knew exactly when it was. It was the day before when Victoria had given her the two whips, and then Kuna's big muscled body moved in response to her body, to her hands and her brain and her willpower. Somehow, his nerve system had connected with hers. She knew now she could ride again.

And with Ben around, she no longer had to depend on her mother to drive her places. Often now, after physio, she and Ben went out for coffee or lunch. Suddenly she had a life. Sort of a life.

And a friend. But she couldn't quite figure Ben out. He was warm and friendly on the surface but any time she asked him questions about his life, he clammed up. He had been friendly, talkative even about a few things, but that was it. Not that she expected any romantic moves on his part. Maybe he just needed a friend. Someone to talk to or spend time with. He didn't seem to have his own friends that she knew about. She had asked him a few polite questions about high school and had gotten a distinct, "Let's not go there" reaction. So she hadn't. They talked about horses, or about her life before the accident. They went for lunch, or for walks in the park. It was great but she still wondered why he was hanging around with her and not with friends his own age.

Willy was finishing her homework. She lay back on the bed watching the sun playing on the leaves of the big maple tree outside her window. The phone rang. Her mother answered, said something, and hung up. She knocked on the door of Willy's room.

"Ben wants to know if you want to go have ice cream this afternoon. He says there's no school today. It's the teachers' professional day."

"Sure," she said. Maybe she could ask Ben about schedules for swimming and the gym.

At two o'clock, Ben picked her up. But once in the car Willy realized she had kind of forgotten that she didn't want to see anyone from her school. On a normal day, at two in the afternoon, everyone should have been in school. They shouldn't have been there at the ice cream shop, the gaggle of girls, three of them, ordering coffees and giggling together.

"Willy," one of them screamed. "Willy, where have you been all this time? Oh my gawd, I thought you had, like, died or something."

"Hi Suzanne, hi Elly, Justine."

They crowded around her and then sat in the red plastic booth with her and Ben without being invited. Questions barraged her. "So are you, like, okay? Are you coming back to school? Oh my God, is that your wheelchair? How do you stand it? Stuck in that thing all day. I would just die!"

It was even worse than she had imagined. She introduced them to Ben. They had all seen him in school but he was older than they were. They ate their ice cream and gossiped about who was going out with who and who had said what to who. As she listened and said nothing, Willy suddenly felt old and tired. She had been like this once, not very long ago.

She had giggled and gossiped and then the accident had cut her life in two.

"Sorry, I've really got to go. Ben, I promised my mom we'd be home."

Ben, who knew perfectly well she had done no such thing, said, "Right, I didn't notice the time. Yeah, we gotta get going. Nice to meet you all."

With gritted teeth, Willy waited for Ben to come around, get her out of the booth and into the wheelchair. The three girls fell absolutely silent, watching her. When she sat down in the wheelchair, she looked at the girls. "So nice to see you," she said. "Have a really, really great day."

And then Ben wheeled her out of the restaurant. She could hear them, already talking about her, not even bothering to lower their voices.

"Oh, my God," she heard Suzanne say. "Did you ever see anything so brave? How does she stand it?" And then something more that Willy didn't catch because the door was already open, and Ben had wheeled her through it.

When they were in the car, he turned to her.

"That wasn't so bad, was it?"

She was shaking. She clenched her hands and looked at him. "It was worse than I thought it would be. It was horrible. I was so right to not go back to school. They felt sorry for me. They thought I was a freak."

"Not everyone is like that."

Willy was silent. Then she said, "Maybe that's true. But how can I tell?"

"Oh come on, Willy, you can't shut yourself away the rest of your life. It's not right. Lots of people have stuff to deal with. You're not that unusual."

She looked out the window. "Just take me home." Right now she never wanted to leave her house again, and she certainly didn't want to see Ben again until she had recovered from being so completely embarrassed in front of him.

That night, she lay on the bed and texted her friend, Lailla. Lailla's parents had moved to Canada from India before Lailla was born. They were both doctors. Lailla had long black hair that she wore in a braid down her back. She was shy and quiet except with Willy. Willy hadn't seen Lailla much since the accident. Because Willy hadn't felt like visiting when Lailla had asked to come over, Willy hadn't responded. After a while, Lailla stopped asking.

Once, they had been best friends. Maybe, Willy thought, even though she had been so rude, something was still left of their friendship. She and Lailla had met in grade seven, in their first year of high school. They had sat beside each other in all their classes. They had giggled their way down the halls of the school and walked home together.

"Hi Lailla," she typed. "Are you there?"

The answer came back almost instantly. "I'm here. So you are still alive. I heard rumours but I wasn't sure."

In spite of herself, Willy smiled. Lailla always had a wicked sense of sarcasm.

"Sorry, I just wasn't up to talking to anyone for a while. I felt like crap."

"So what's changed?"

"I'm getting better. By the way, I saw some girls at the ice cream shop today. Suzanne, Ellie and Justine. They made me so mad I had to talk to someone."

"Oh, yes, the three evil witches. Bet they had some lovely remarks. Girl, I should be so mad at you but I am just so glad to hear from you that I forgot it already. How the heck are you?"

"Okay. Still in a wheelchair. But I am learning to move my legs. A little."

"Well, if anyone can beat this crappy crap, it is you!!!! Despite the fact that you have IGNORED me except for the occasional text, I believe in you. And I am still your friend. Crazy, I know. I've been texting you but you never answer."

"I know. I'm so sorry. Thanks for staying in touch," Willy typed. "I am your friend too. For a while, I thought I didn't need friends and I just wanted to be alone, but I met this guy, Ben. Then today he really pissed me off, plus those girls totally embarrassed me in front of him. I don't know whether I want to see him again now or not. Hard to look him in the eye after listening to them go on about how pitiful I am."

"Well, my goodness, a guy! That would be very, very cool. Of course I want to meet him."

"JUST FRIENDS, I SAID," Willy typed. "He goes to our school. He's in grade eleven. He's nice but I think he just feels sorry for me. He's kind of strange. He's friendly but distant too. I can't quite figure him out."

"No way he feels sorry for you. Don't be silly. I am sure he likes you a lot. You're fun to hang with when you're not being a reclusive bitch."

"Well, gee thanks, I guess."

"So what are you so mad about?"

"He basically told me to quit feeling sorry for myself. He's right but it made me so mad to hear him."

"Hmm. That's a tough one. None of his business how you feel about things."

"Yeah, but he made me think. By the way, thanks for waiting for me to quit feeling sorry for myself. I didn't know if you were still talking to me."

"You're so totally welcome. BFFs, remember. Hey gotta go . . . Mom is paging me. TTYL. I'll message you back after I find out what she wants. I am going to call you so we can really talk!"

Willy stared at the phone. Suddenly she was restless. And bored. But tomorrow was riding day. Tomorrow.

She wheeled herself out of her room. "Mom, can I ask you something?"

"Yes, of course, honey."

"I know I said I hated swimming."

"Yes?"

"But I want to start going twice a week. And to the gym."

"Yeah, sure, good ideas. I'll check the schedule, see when it's open. Do you want to go to the public swim or sign up for a class?"

"I want to go when no one else is there."

Her mom gave her a look. "Right. Well, there must be times when the place is mostly empty. I'll check that out. I know the woman that works at the office. I'll give her a call."

Chapter 8

"SIT UP STRAIGHT. Heels down. Hands, yes, very nice. That looks good. Fine, walk on, please."

Willy squeezed her legs as hard as she could. She could feel the muscles in her legs move. Kuna stepped out obediently. She still had the two dressage whips but this time he had moved just from the pressure of her legs.

She felt stronger after every ride. Somehow, riding the horse also moved her hips, arms, shoulders, hands, legs and feet so that they all began to work together. Victoria had explained it all to her one day and had loaned her a film about it as well. "The horse moves your body as if you were walking," she had said. "So it wakes up all your working nerves and muscles and strengthens them as well."

Plus when she was on a horse, she wasn't crippled. She was strong, fast, tall, capable.

"Okay, this afternoon, I want you to try to move into a rising trot, then sitting trot, then walk," Victoria said. "I know it is really hard for you to stand in the stirrups so don't try to stand. Just let his movement throw you up a bit and then come down again. It's just a small movement. Don't overdo it."

Concentrate, Willy thought. She nudged the horse with her heel and he obediently picked up a trot. She tried to let the motion of the horse move her own body into the rise and fall of the motion. After several transitions between walk and trot, her legs were aching but she knew she had done it. She had gone up and down with the motion of the horse. Her legs were strong enough to hold her up, even though they couldn't lift her up. It all felt so familiar. It felt great. She grinned at Victoria.

"Good transition into the walk," Victoria said. "But you're letting him get too heavy in front. Pick up your reins. Drive him on a bit. Tap him with the whips. That's what they are for."

They went back at it. When the lesson was over, Victoria came to lead her out of the ring. Kuna parked himself obediently right beside the wheelchair ramp. Willy slid her legs out of the stirrups, then Elizabeth, who was standing on the other side of Kuna, helped her lever one leg over the saddle, until she was lying belly down on the saddle, both legs dangling down one side. She let go, slid off Kuna, while Victoria was right there behind her. Still, her legs almost collapsed under her. Ben was right there with the wheelchair but she went on standing, holding onto the saddle.

"I want to try something. Turn the wheelchair so I can hold onto it," Willy said. Everyone stared at her for a moment and then Ben turned the wheelchair so the handles were in front of her. Willy clenched her muscles and concentrated until she felt the impulse in her leg. Her muscles contracted and the heel of her right foot came up until she could drag her toes forward. Then she stood on that foot, picked up the other foot, the muscles in her legs clenching and un-clenching. She gritted her teeth, lurched forward, and almost fell. She stood panting, her hands on the wheelchair handles.

Victoria looked at her. "I've got an idea, too. Ben, please tie up Kuna and then come back. Willy, can you go on standing there?"

Willy nodded. She stood for a few moments until Kuna was tied.

"Okay, now, Elizabeth and Ben, please come here," Victoria said. "Ben, take one of her arms. Elizabeth, you take the other."

Victoria moved the wheelchair aside and held out her hands. Willy grabbed Victoria's hands with her own. Then slowly but steadily, with Elizabeth and Ben on either side, she walked by standing on one leg and then dragging the other leg forward, then the next, painfully slow, step by step. At three steps, she decided to stop. Her legs were shaking. Sharp pains slid up the muscles as if someone were poking her with hot wires. It was more than she had ever thought she could do.

She collapsed into the wheelchair, and Victoria wheeled her beside Kuna and handed her a brush.

"Soon," Willy said to Victoria. "I'm doing it all myself. I am going to saddle my own horse and lead him into the ring."

"Good idea," Victoria said calmly.

"I'm not going to stay a cripple," Willy said.

"No, you're not."

"I'm going to walk again."

"You're already walking. What do you call what you just accomplished?"

"Better."

"Yes, you will do better. You are doing better every week. I can see the change in you. We all can."

"I want to ride competitively, I want to ride a dressage test. I want to jump again. I want to be who I was. I am not staying a crippled rider."

"Sure, sounds good." Victoria bent to clean Kuna's feet. "When you're ready. You're not ready yet though."

"I know. My legs aren't strong enough."

"I thought he responded pretty well to your legs today. He picked up his trot whenever you asked him. You both looked good out there." Victoria put Kuna's hind leg down, straightened up, and looked at Willy. "I think you are doing really well. Don't you? There's no hurry. As long as you are continuing to get well, that is all that matters. And look what you did today. You walked. Three steps!"

Willy sighed. "All I can think about is how it used to be. How I used to ride. What I used to do. I just want it all back."

"Well, that's probably pretty normal. That's probably a good way to feel. It's what drives you to try so hard. But you also need to be glad for what you have achieved."

"Yeah, I know. Everybody says I'm supposed to adjust, I'm supposed to be patient, and get used to being this way. I hate it! I just want things to go back the way they were. I hate being the crippled girl. The one everybody feels sorry for."

"Yes, I'm sure you do. But in the meantime, I'm thinking that in the next couple of weeks we could move into trot-canter transitions. What do you think? Can you handle it? Kuna has a very well-balanced canter. Would you be nervous?"

"No way," Willy said. "Let's do it. That would be great."

"Willy," Victoria said. "The whole core of your body is getting stronger, not just your legs. You walk with your whole body."

"Yeah, that is what my physio said."

"So what would you think about riding twice a week?"

"I would love it!"

Even as she shouted it out, she began thinking of Ben, and what he thought of her new excitement. Until now she had talked to him mostly about her frustration, about her black moods, and about how her parents drove her crazy by hovering over her. Although she had tried to keep it light, as she didn't want him to think she was just some spoiled brat that was always depressed, her illness had been in large part the basis for their friendship.

There was his own illness, of course, but he rarely mentioned it. She knew it hurt him sometimes. She had seen him wince folding up the wheelchair. Seen him limp when he thought no one was looking. She'd be so glad when she was stronger and not a burden on him anymore. She felt bad every time he had to drive her somewhere, every time he had to lift her in and out of the car. She wanted now to show him that she really was a strong person, that she could be independent and together. Maybe then she could let herself think, just a little, that there might be more going on here than just friendship. At the moment, she told herself, they were friends. Good friends and that was all it could ever be until she could walk again. She turned her mind away from this treacherous emotional bog. Later, she thought. She'd deal with it all later.

When they got to Ben's car and he halted the wheelchair beside the door, she said, "Let me try it on my own." Slowly she levered herself out of the wheelchair, opened the car door, twisted her body so that she could fall into the passenger seat. She had to lift her legs in one at a time with her hands, but she did it and then she shut the door and triumphantly put on her seat belt. She felt totally exhausted, as if she had run a marathon.

Ben put the wheelchair in the trunk as always, then got in the driver's side. Without a word, he started the car and drove out of the parking lot. When they were on the highway, he drove too fast, staring straight ahead. At first Willy didn't pay any attention, she was so excited about what had just happened. Her heart was still pumping fast.

"That was so great," she said. "Oh, Ben, I can't believe I just did that. Plus walking. All that in one day! And I can do a sitting trot. Did you see me? And soon Victoria is going to let us canter. That is so great."

"Yeah, you're on your way now for sure. You'll be jumping and running races soon."

"I used to be on the school basketball team, did I tell you?"

"Nope, I'm sure you were the dancing queen too."

"Ben, what's the matter?" Willy asked finally. "Why are you driving so fast? Slow down."

In response, he drove even faster. He passed several cars that he shouldn't have. Willy couldn't help it. She closed her eyes, said loudly, "Ben stop it, stop, please stop." The car slowed. She opened her eyes. "I'm sorry, the accident, it brings it all back when you go so fast."

"Oh right, sorry, Willy, I'm so sorry." There was a gravel pullout beside the road and he braked, pulled in and stopped. "I forgot. I guess I was . . . I don't know, zoned out or something."

"I thought you were mad about something."

"It was nothing. Forget it. Just something that happened

earlier. I had an argument with my dad. Sometimes, he just doesn't get it. He doesn't get me. He doesn't even know who I am." He paused. Willy didn't say anything. Her heart was still pounding. She felt slightly sick. All she wanted to do was go home. She knew she should ask him what he had fought with his dad about but her legs hurt.

"So when are you going back to school, hang out with all your friends?" Ben asked.

"What? I told you, I'm not going back to school."

"Well, except now you can walk and all. You'll be wanting your social life back. Hanging out at Dairy Queen, going to the mall." She looked at him. His eyes were shiny with unshed tears. He smiled at her but it was not the smile of anyone she knew.

"I don't know if I'm ever going back to school. Look, Ben, I really don't want to have this conversation right now. And I don't hang out at Dairy Queen. What are you talking about? I was feeling so good. Now I just want to go home, please."

"Fine," he said. "Just great. Don't talk to me then."

They drove home in silence. Ben drove too slowly and too carefully. Willy stared out the window. What had just happened? She should have been feeling so happy. She had ridden well, she had walked down the ramp on her own, she had climbed in and out of the car by herself. All good. So what was with Ben?

Once he pulled the car into the driveway, he seemed to recover. He climbed out, lifted out the wheelchair, helped her into it and pushed her to the door. When Willy's mom opened the door, he smiled. "Here she is, safe and sound," he said cheerfully. "Gotta run or I'll be late for dinner."

Dinner? It was barely five o'clock. She stared at him. He gave her a strange twisted smile, whirled around, jumped in the car and left. Weird, she decided. Weird she could do without. Her life was difficult enough.

"Such a nice young man," her mother said, too cheerful as always. "How was your ride, sweetie? You look so pretty today."

Willy sighed. Just when she was on the verge of forgiving her mother for trying too hard and hoping too much, her mother said something dumb, and she got mad at her all over again. She decided not to tell her mother about those three steps down the ramp after she slid off Kuna. She couldn't face the deluge of hope and cheerfulness she knew it would bring. But she would have to tell her sometime. Or her mother would probably find out from Victoria.

"Willy, dinner will be ready early tonight. It's just you and Em. You're in charge. Your dad and I are going out. It's our anniversary. We're going to celebrate."

"Out? You're actually going out. Hallelujah. Where?"

"Some really crazy new diner place your dad picked out. It's like a sixties' throwback place. It's been a while since we had time together." Willy could see the new lines of worry etched in her mother's face, and a streak of grey in her hair that hadn't been there before her accident. Her mom looked weird. She was wearing blue jeans and a red scarf and red high-heeled shoes. To go out to dinner? Really?

Willy wheeled herself over the doorsill, down the hall to her room, went into her room and sat in front of the computer. She felt her stomach twist. She wheeled her way back out into the hall. Her mother was just coming down the stairs, swinging a jean jacket over her shoulders.

"Willy, are you hungry already?"

"Mom, I am going to show you something but only if you promise to be calm, okay? Don't start jumping up and down or anything."

"What? I am always calm, Willy. What do you mean, jumping? I would never do such a thing."

"Then come here and just stand beside me, okay?"

"Sure."

Her mother walked over and stood beside the wheelchair, and Willy used the arms to lever herself to her feet. She stood straight and then she wrapped her arm through her mother's for balance.

"Okay," Willy said, "one step, please, slowly, and then another."

Her mother looked at her.

"Walk," Willy said softly. "Take one step."

Her mother stepped forward and Willy repeated her earlier movement of dragging her heel off the floor and then commanding her leg muscles to lift up and over and down again. Only now it was harder because her leg muscles, she discovered, were tired and sore from the earlier exercise. She managed three steps this time before she had to sit down again.

As Willy collapsed into the wheelchair, her mother put her face in her hands and then looked up, a smile lighting up her whole face. "Willy, I knew you could do it. I just knew it. I told your dad you would."

"You did?"

"I heard you one night. I saw your light was on and I peeked in your room. I saw you standing up. I didn't want to say anything. It was obvious that you wanted to keep it secret. Oh honey, I am so proud of you."

She came over and hugged Willy and Willy hugged her back.

"Sweetie, let me call your dad."

Willy's dad came down the stairs. For once he wasn't wearing a suit. He was wearing a sweater instead. And blue jeans. And running shoes. Really?

"Willy, I saw you," he said. "I was watching from the top of the stairs. You did it, you did it," he said. He couldn't speak any more because his voice choked. Willy felt suddenly totally exhausted. Walking on top of riding and now her weepy parents. Too much. She needed a shower. And supper. And a chance to chat with Lailla.

"Just go, you two, you look so cool!" she said. "I need a rest. And some food. Go on, they'll give your table to someone else."

She ate dinner with Emily, a macaroni and cheese casserole their mom had left in the oven, with a salad and apple juice.

After dinner, on the computer, she Skyped Lailla and asked her what people at school thought of Ben.

"He's weird," Lailla said. "He's hanging out with the wrong people. He's trouble, Willy, stay away from him."

"I thought we were friends and then today he was so strange. He was driving too fast. He said he had a fight with his dad or something like that. And I was so excited because I walked. I really did. I did it, Lailla. I am getting better. It's riding. It's made me strong. I am so excited."

"And I'm happy for you too. Hey, when are you going to run over to my house?"

"Soon, my friend, soon. Watch for me from your window. I'll come jogging by."

Next week, Ben didn't call to ask her if she wanted him to pick her up to go to the riding centre. Willy waited. She was not going to call him. Her mom drove her.

After riding, Willie slid off Kuna, and this time, with Victoria's help again, she managed four steps. Then together she and Victoria brushed Kuna and put him away. Victoria stood with her while Willie waited for her mom. "Seen Ben today?" Victoria asked. "He didn't show up for riding and he didn't phone. It's not like him."

"He was upset last week," Willy said. "He said he had a fight with his dad."

"Hmm, maybe I should call him? I don't quite know what He's usually so reliable. But there's only two weeks of riding left for this session, so I guess I'll see if he shows up next week."

"Only two weeks left? Wow, I hadn't noticed. I knew it was going to be over soon but I didn't want to think about it."

"The horses and I both need a summer holiday. It's hot. It's been a busy spring. We've had more riders than ever. We'll start up again the last week of August. You need the summer off too. But if you see Ben, tell him to call me."

"I'd ride every day if I could," Willy said. She didn't say anything about Ben. She had no idea what to say.

When her mom picked her up, Willy slid into the car from her mom's arms. "Only two more weeks left," she said. "And I feel as if I'm just getting started. Kuna and I are really connecting. We're a team now."

"It's just a break," her mom said. "Doesn't riding start up again in September? Your dad and I are thinking about renting a cabin on the lake for August. We could stay out there all of August and you could swim every day. I wonder if Lailla would like to come, too?"

With riding out of her life, Willy had time on her hands. It was July and hot and she was restless. Ben seemed to have disappeared entirely out of her life. She decided he had dumped their friendship and she felt too proud to call him. But Lailla had reappeared, and Willy and Lailla spent long hours in the backyard at Willy's house, hanging out, gossiping, catching up on everyone at school.

Every week, at physiotherapy, Willy practised walking. She

went swimming at the local pool twice a week. Lailla went with her and they tried to find times to go when they knew that no one from the high school was likely to be there. But this became more difficult because many of their classmates from the school were either practising or competing in swimming competitions and were often at the pool. They made a gleeful point of passing Lailla and Willy, calling loud greetings, snickering at each other sometimes.

Willy said hi back, politely. These people used to be her friends. She used to play basketball with some of them. She used to run into the washroom with them, giggling over the latest gossip. They had gone all the way through school together, from preschool to high school.

Now, somehow, they couldn't see her properly. They said, "Hi, Willy," and then their eyes slid past her as if she were someone they used to know a long time ago but now could barely remember. It made her furiously angry but there wasn't much she could do. What she wanted to do was get out of the pool, march down to the end where they were all lined up near the diving board, and say something really mean, nasty, and pissed off and then spin around and march away again. Or yell at them as they walked by. "Hey it's me, remember when we played together?" But of course she didn't say anything.

Instead, she stayed beside Lailla in the kiddie pool, doing her exercises. The good thing about the exercises was that they were working. Her legs were getting a little bit stronger every week. Willy did knee bends, stretches and practised walking with the water as support. Then Lailla helped Willy back into the wheelchair and helped her change into her street clothes.

July slid by and August showed up.

"Time to go to the cabin, kiddos," said Willy's father one night over dinner. "Time to pack. Time to blow the dust of this town out of our ears."

Willy stared at him. "Are you coming with us?" she asked. Usually in the summer their dad took a few days off, or if they rented a cabin at the lake out of town, he came out on weekends but he still stayed in town to work during the week.

"Three weeks," he said. "Three weeks at the lake. It's time for a break with my three favourite girls. Get the cobwebs out of my head. What do you think?"

"Yay, Daddy," yelled Emily. She jumped out of her chair, ran around the table and threw herself into her dad's lap.

Willy looked at her mom who smiled and shrugged. "Sounds good to me." Willy looked at her dad. He was teasing Emily, pretending to tickle her, mussing her hair while she screamed in mock fear and delight. Something had changed in her family. Something big.

"Can Lailla come with us?" Willy asked.

"Sure, Willy, why not. Emily, do you want to bring your friend as well?"

And so summer began. Willy's mother, of course, packed way too much stuff but that didn't matter. Willy didn't care.

All she wanted to take was her bathing suit, a towel and her toothbrush.

The cabin sat just above a small but private sandy beach on a big lake. They could swim, or there were canoes and a place to have a bonfire on the beach at night.

Her physiotherapist had given her two canes. "Try walking with these," she said. Willy tried but it seemed hopeless. The only way she could walk was by either hanging on to the back of the wheelchair or with Lailla holding her on one side and her mother on the other. And even then it hurt. A lot.

Willy started to relax. She didn't have to worry about people staring or wondering what was wrong with her. But it was awkward getting from the cabin to the beach because her wheelchair wouldn't go over the rough sandy ground.

One day, with Lailla on one side and her mother on the other, she tried to walk with the canes, limping and lurching from side to side. She felt ridiculous. Lailla and her mother half-supported, half-carried her into the water. The next day she tried it again.

"Let me do it myself," she said. She shook off their helpful restraining hands and stood still for a moment, picturing the movements. It was all so complicated. Swing one cane forward and lean her weight on that cane. Drag that foot forward. Lean her weight forward onto that foot. Swing the other cane forward. Lean on that cane. Drag that foot forward. Put her weight on that foot. Wait for the sharp knife-like pain shooting through her leg to subside. Then repeat the whole routine. Keep going. Keep going. Right to the water's edge.

Swimming was her reward. In the water, she pulled herself along with her arms and used her legs only for balance. The water was soft and cool and while swimming, she was light, relaxed, agile.

She forgot about Ben and about school. Now, during the day, she and Lailla lounged on the beach or ate picnic food. At night, Willy and Lailla lay in their bunk beds in the cabin and talked late until her mother finally came to the door of their room and begged them to go to sleep.

During the day, Willy's dad lay in the water on an inflated inner tube, his ancient ball cap pulled over his eyes. Or he went for walks. He read books.

And then one day, far too soon, it was almost September. They were lying on the beach in the hot August sun when Lailla reminded her. "Are you coming back to school in September?" she asked dreamily, her face pillowed on the towel.

Willy turned her head and stared at her friend. "No way."

"It would be so great to have you back," Lailla said. "It's lonely without you. When the three witches show up, I have to hide out. I just go to the library and read."

Willy's mom had persuaded Lailla to get a haircut so now her hair was a short and silky bob. She was wearing a bright yellow bathing suit which looked wonderful against her brown skin.

Willy's parents had invited Lailla's parents to the cabin for dinner but they never came. When Willy asked Lailla why, she shrugged. "They're doctors. They're crazy busy. They don't really have time to have friends."

Thinking over Lailla's question about school, Willy said, "Sorry, Lailla, I just can't go back to school. I don't want people looking at me and making stupid remarks and feeling sorry for me. Everyone else will be playing basketball and hanging out. I was the basketball team captain, remember."

"Yep, you were the star player, no question," Lailla said. "But I don't feel sorry for you. I think you are totally amazing. When my parents and I saw you in the hospital, the doctors told us you would probably never walk again. And look at you. Every day you look a little stronger. You walk a little straighter. And now you're going riding again. It's all so cool. I mean you are still the star. All you have to do at school is show up. C'mon, it'll be okay. I hate it there by myself."

Willy thought about it. She knew she was being selfish. "I'm just not ready, Lailla. I can't face it. I just can't. But I will, as soon as I am ready. I promise. You will be the first to know."

Lailla sighed. "Okay, I won't bug you about it. Are you going to see that Ben guy again?"

"I don't know. He hasn't called. Guess I was just a pity party for him. You know, help the poor crippled girl for a bit until you grow tired of it."

"He's weird. Sometimes he hangs out with those druggie dudes who smoke at the back of the school but they don't really seem to be his friends. They're people he's with now and then. Maybe he's just lonely, too."

"Don't know. Don't care." She lay back down on her towel. Ben, school, riding, all the problems she had put away for the summer were now wide awake and jumping in her brain.

That night, she and Lailla talked long into the night about school, about whether or not Lailla could also drop out and do home schooling with Willy and what they both really wanted to do with their lives.

"I'd love to quit school, Willy, but my parents would never let me," Lailla whispered. "They already have my career planned out. They want me to be a doctor but I really want to be a writer."

"Girls, please go to sleep," Willy's mother called. Soon the cabin was peaceful. But Willy lay awake for a long time, the ideas about what they both might do in the future going around and around in her head.

Chapter 9

"Willy, I've got a surprise for you," Victoria said. She led the way down the line of stalls towards the end. Willy came behind her in the wheelchair. She was now alternating time in the wheelchair with time walking with the canes. Since summer, her progress had been slow but steady. As long as she was on firm level ground, she could walk very slowly, standing up straight, with a long hesitation in each step as she picked up each foot and put it down again. But when she got too tired and her legs hurt too much, she still used the wheelchair.

At the end of the line of stalls, a dark brown head with a

white blaze poked out. Big brown eyes looked at them. "His name is Sand," Victoria said. "Well, that's his stable name. His real name is Sanderson Victorio. But Sand is a good name for him. It means grit, tough, strong. And he is that. He's ten years old, trained to dressage and jumping. But he's a rescue horse. I really don't know what to do with him. Elizabeth brought him to us because his owners were going to have him put down. He was hurt last year. He escaped from the barn, somehow. And then he was out on the highway in the middle of the night and was hit by a truck. The truck tire went over his foot. He had to stand in a stall for a year while his hoof grew back. His owner didn't think he would ever be really well.

"The problem is, ever since he got hit, he spooks at things. Apparently he's okay in the ring but out on trails, you never know when he's going to panic and bolt. He's already thrown a couple of good riders. His owner was moving, and she was afraid he wouldn't go to a good home, or even worse, go to a meat buyer, so she was going to have him put down humanely. But Elizabeth thought he was too good a horse to be put down like that. As I say, I don't know what to do with him. He's not really the kind of horse we can use here. We're just keeping him here until we can find him a home with someone who can handle him. Plus he needs a lot of walking to get back in shape."

"He's so beautiful," Willy said. "Can I go in the stall with him?"

"No, let me lead him out. I want to have another look at him anyway. I guess we will have to try and sell him but he might never be really sound or safe for anyone to ride. Here, wait just a minute."

Victoria opened the stall door, slipped a halter on Sand's head, and led him out. He put his head up and neighed loudly. "He can be a bit of a handful apparently, when he feels like it," she said. "But he's a good mover. The leg seems fine now but hard to say if it would stand up to riding. I've seen him in action at shows before he got hurt. He loves to jump."

Willy stared at him in admiration. He was a warm dark chocolate brown all over, except for the blaze on his head and one slip of white on his hind foot. Willy put out her hand; he sniffed, then threw his head up to whinny again.

"I thought you'd like to have a look at him, see what a Grand Prix dressage horse looks like. I rode him yesterday," Victoria said. "Just took him for a walk. He was fine, very well behaved. I'll keep riding him for a while and see if he's going to be a good boy. And then we'll have to figure out what to do with him. I can't afford to have him just hanging around here. This place runs on a shoestring at the best of times. I don't have funding for a rescue horse. Okay, I'm going to turn him out in the field for a bit. Then let's get you up on Kuna and work on those transitions."

After she let Sand go into the field, Victoria pushed Willy in her wheelchair to Kuna's stall. After Victoria brought him out and tied him, Willy and Victoria brushed Kuna, then saddled and bridled him. Victoria led Kuna to the mounting ramp, while Elizabeth pushed Willy up the ramp. Then Willy stood up from her wheelchair, put one foot in a stirrup, raised her other leg over the saddle, and slid, slowly and carefully, onto Kuna's back and sat upright. It was the first time she had mounted her horse with no one lifting her into the saddle. She and Kuna walked around the ring. Willy took deep breaths. Her first ride of the season. Her body felt stiff and uncoordinated.

"Centre, relax," called Victoria. "Deep breaths. Head up. Shoulders back. Look where you are going."

Kuna had a long stride at a walk but when Willy tightened the reins a bit and squeezed with her legs, he sprang into a trot that surprised her with its strength. Victoria coached and instructed from the centre of the ring. After doing several lengths of the ring at a trot, Willy put her outside leg back and Kuna obediently picked up his canter. Willy was exhilarated. She sat up straight and felt her body move to the familiar rocking rhythm. She braced her back, felt Kuna obediently slow and gather his muscled body under her. She felt as if she and Kuna were finally really a team. Feeling the strength come back into her legs had been the key and all the swimming and walking she had done over the summer had made a huge difference.

At the end of the lesson, she let the reins go slack and Kuna stretched his head down as she rode into the centre of the ring. Victoria met her there. "That was great," she said briskly.

"Slide off and we'll put him away together and then let's have a chat."

When Kuna was finally unsaddled and brushed, with Willy and Victoria working quietly together, Victoria said, "Okay, come over here." They sat together at the table-and-chair set at one end of the riding ring. "I want to ask if you would consider training for a para-equestrian dressage competition?"

"Maybe," Willy said cautiously.

"You wouldn't have to travel. We can video your test and send it in."

"So who would I be competing with?"

"Well, other riders all across the country with various levels of disability."

"No way," said Willy. "If I'm going to compete, I want to go in a regular show."

"Willy, I think you will find this competition pretty satisfying. You would be competing with other athletes at your level of disability. Someone will come from the para-equestrian riding association to assess your riding ability. Here's their website. It's on this letter. Go home and look it up. Look at some of the videos of their riders. Look at what para-equestrians can do. Canada has some of the best para-equestrian riders in the world. I think you'll be impressed."

"Is this the same kind of competition that Ben does?"

"Yes, Ben used to be one of our best riders. But he didn't come in for this session. He never even called. Maybe he has outgrown riding. Lost interest. People do. It's sad. But I'm sure he has a good reason." She frowned then said, "I think you would do very well in competition."

That night Willy sat in front of her computer and watched video after video of para-equestrians riding, people who sat their horses with grace and skill. Some people rode their horses even though they couldn't walk. Some rode with no arms. She began to feel a kind of excitement she hadn't felt for a long time. She could do this, she thought. She could really do this, and do it well. She remembered the sense of power and control she had during this afternoon's ride.

"All right," said Willy under her breath. It was a new beginning, she thought to herself. Another huge step on the road to being well. If she had to compete with other people who were also disabled, she would. That was fair. For now. And one day she would compete at the highest level she could reach. Crippled or not.

When she woke in the mornings now, she had a reason to get up. She was training, she told herself. In training. For a competition. What a word. She still forgot some mornings that she couldn't walk properly and she still, just before she really woke up, expected to jump out of bed.

She still remembered, vividly, what that felt like, that rush of anticipation, of moving. She dreamed it. She woke from dreams of playing basketball, of skiing, of running.

The dreams, in some ways, were worse now that she could move her legs. When she had been paralyzed, she could take refuge in bitterness, in despair and dreams of a sad, lonely, noble death.

But now there was hope, and yet the gap between who she had been and who she was still felt so much bigger than she could deal with. What she needed now was patience, and that she didn't have. Shuffling along on a couple of canes, dragging each foot, one at a time, teeth gritted, still made her feel like some kind of grotesque clown. No matter what she wore or how she did her hair. Or that she could ride.

She could see, far down the road, the possibility of getting almost well, a place where she might look and feel normal. A place where she could walk in a room and no one would turn to stare. Or feel sorry for her. Or say, with that particular cheeriness, "Oh hi, Willy, how are you?" not wanting her to answer, or really tell them, the question only a pretense of compassion.

In some ways, it was that little piece of shining hope that made it harder. Because she still had to close that gap. And she wasn't sure how long it would take, or if she could really do it.

She had also spent a long time thinking about Sand. She had gone to the library and taken out several books on training and horsemanship, as well as doing further research at home on the Internet. She came across several theories that involved spending time with the horse, taking him outside, letting him lead a more natural life.

She knew Victoria had only shown Sand to her out of interest. She hadn't meant Willy to put any energy into the horse. But Willy decided to ask Victoria if she could work with him a little bit, maybe take him for walks, spend time with him, gain his confidence and try to give him a different life. He was such a beautiful horse and it was so unfair that he had been crippled, too. Maybe, if and when he grew calmer, she could even try riding him.

Two things now made it worthwhile getting out of bed: riding Kuna and a chance to work with Sand.

"If you're going to compete," Victoria had told her, "you need to ride at least twice a week. Or more."

She would have gone every day if she could. But twice a week was great. And Kuna and she were becoming a real team. The week after Sand arrived, she asked Victoria if they could talk.

"Sure," Victoria said. "Let's sit down. Tell me what's on your mind."

"I've been reading about ideas that I think will help Sand. I wanted to ask you if I could start working with him one-on-one so he has a person that he learns to trust. Take him for walks. Spend time with him. I think he needs to get back to just being a normal horse. And then we would have to go right back to basics with his training. Start all over again." She looked nervously at Victoria.

Victoria sighed deeply. "Willy, he's not your problem. I've been trying to figure out what to do about Sand, too. I can't afford to keep him here. And you're right. He needs retraining so I can find a buyer for him. And now that he doesn't need to stand in a stall, he can stay out on the pasture and get used to being a horse again. He can stay in the backfield for now. But I just don't have enough time to deal with him."

"That's okay. I can do it."

"I don't think so. He's not safe for you to handle by yourself. Your sense of balance still needs work. Plus you have the canes to deal with. Leading a horse with two canes would be a real challenge. You could fall, or he could shy at the canes. No, it's just not safe."

"I am just going to hang out with him. Take him for slow walks. Get him used to me. He needs a person he can trust."

"Hmm. Yes, that is true." She stared at Willy. "You're really determined about this, aren't you? Well, we can try it once, see how it goes. So, okay, yes, you can work with him as long as someone else is with you. But if I can find another home for him, out he goes."

So now Willy spent some time with Sand every time she went to the stables. If she could get Elizabeth or one of the other volunteers to walk beside her, she took him for very slow walks, using her canes, his halter rope looped over one arm. She let him graze and look around. The walking was good for her too. So far, he had been completely calm. Sometimes, when she went to put him back in the field, or in his stall, he would shove his warm brown head into her chest while she scratched under his chin and behind his ears. They would lean in close together, as if he were asking her for reassurance. She held his head and they breathed together and then Elizabeth led him into his stall.

But Ben ... Ben was becoming an even bigger mystery. He had phoned her just after riding began again and asked if he could drive her to the riding centre. He apologized for his behaviour. He hadn't called, he said, because he had been away. When he came to pick her up and drive her to the riding centre, he was perfectly normal and polite. A little too polite. Too nice. Or something. Something she couldn't put her finger on. He seemed as if he were pretending to be Ben, a replica of the real Ben somehow.

She was genuinely glad to see him. She tried to talk to him, and when he didn't answer or just gave monosyllabic answers, she gave up, puzzled, and stared out the window while he drove.

So why had he called if he didn't want to talk? Maybe he had a girlfriend she didn't know about. Maybe they laughed together about the poor crippled girl he was being nice to. Helping her out.

Well, she'd never asked him to help her. It was he who had barged into her life, he who had volunteered to help. In fact, she had been pretty rude to him at first. So if he didn't want to be bothered with her anymore, that would be just fine.

They drove in silence to the riding centre. Previously, he had always come in with her, but today he simply helped her out of the car and then leaned against the car door while she made her wobbly way, leaning on the two canes, into the stable. This was the first time she had found the courage to leave her wheelchair at home. She had looked forward to being able to show Ben that she could now do without it. Her walk was still wobbly but getting stronger all the time.

Fine, she thought. She'd phone her mom to come and get her.

Her ride didn't go as well as usual. She needed to concentrate completely on herself and her horse, and instead she was too busy fuming at Ben. She could see that Victoria was wondering what was going on. Victoria's voice got a little louder. A couple of times she even stopped Willy, asked her to concentrate. After the lesson, when Kuna was brushed, all the tack cleaned, and Kuna put away in his stall, Victoria beckoned her over to the table.

"Come over here, Willy, there is something I want to tell you."

Willy's heart sank. Was Victoria going to give her a hard time over her riding and her lack of attention?

"Willy, I wanted to talk to you about possible dates for your upcoming video competition. I just received the calendar this morning."

"Great," Willy said.

"I am thinking we should try for this October. But before that, there is a dressage clinic in three weeks for riders from all over the valley. There's a couple of riders coming here who are getting ready to try competing provincially as well. The coach who is coming has ridden on the national Paralympic team. She's just amazing. Her name is Judy Makine. I'd like you to meet her and give her a chance to see how you ride. She was paralyzed and then learned to walk again, partly by riding. I think this would be a fantastic opportunity for you two to meet up."

"Really? Wow, yes, that would be so interesting."

"She wants to meet you as well. I've told her how you are coming along. I think you'll enjoy meeting her, and it will be a chance for the two of you to see how well you are riding. You and Kuna are a good team. Okay, see you next week."

When Willy came outside, Ben was nowhere in sight but his car was still in the parking lot. She hobbled over to it, uncertain of what to do. She had her cell phone. All she had to do was call her mom. She leaned against the car and spotted Ben, coming from one of the rows of stalls where the regular riders kept their horses. When he saw her, he shrugged and said, "Sorry I was late." He opened the door for her but didn't offer any other explanation.

While she was getting in, she exclaimed, "Victoria is organizing a clinic so I can compete this fall in a para-equestrian dressage competition. I am so stoked. If you came back to riding, you could compete too. And there is a dressage clinic in three weeks with this amazing coach who learned to walk after she was paralyzed. And she was on the national para-equestrian team. It will be a fantastic clinic. Want to come?"

"No, I've quit riding," he said.

"What? Why? You are really good. You were the one who talked me into coming here. You said you loved it."

He sighed. "Yeah, well, things change. I have other stuff to do. I wasn't that good anyway."

"Sure you were. Victoria said you were really good. Why did you quit?"

"Oh, nothing. Doesn't matter. I'm doing some other stuff now."

"Like what?" She waited. He looked out the window. Finally she asked cautiously, hating herself for even suggesting it, "Do you want to do something together this week?"

"Do something? Maybe. What do you want to do?"

"I dunno. Hang out. Talk."

He didn't say anything. Then he sighed. "Sure," he said. "Why not?"

"Well, you don't have to sound so enthusiastic about it."

"Sorry."

"Whatever. Just take me home."

When they got to her house, she really wanted to jump out of the car and stomp up the steps and slam the door but she couldn't. She had to struggle out of the car with her two canes. Ben came around to help her and she ignored him. She struggled to stand up and then limped to the door, pulled it open, struggled awkwardly inside, trying not to trip on the doorsill, then once she made it, she slammed the door with a satisfying thunk.

She limped to her room and collapsed on the bed. Well, that was that, she thought. Her life was so pathetic that even someone who felt sorry for her had managed to walk away. Fine. She didn't care. She really, really didn't care. She lost herself in a satisfying daydream of living alone on a huge ranch somewhere with a lot of horses and maybe a dog and no people anywhere at all. She heard the front door thump, and her sister came running and threw herself on the bed.

Then she saw Willy's face. "Willy, what's wrong?"

"Oh nothing. I sort of had a fight with Ben. Only it wasn't a fight because he wouldn't even talk to me."

"Oh wow, that's a drag."

"It doesn't matter. How was your day?"

"Good. I like my new teacher. She's great. I got an A on my story for English. And I have to do my homework right away — Mom said I could go over to Janet's for dinner if I did my homework first. See you."

She bounced up and out of the room. Willy stared after her. Her sister's life was simple and predictable, as hers had been, once. Well, now it would be again. All she would have to do was quit going anywhere, quit riding, quit going out, quit physio. She would sit quietly in her room, not seeing anyone, not going anywhere. Wasn't there some poet lady who had done that, who ended up becoming famous? Maybe she could learn how to write poetry. She didn't feel much like writing poetry, but how hard could it be. She had time on her hands . . . or maybe what she should do is work hard and become a champion rider and when she saw Ben on the street, she could just stomp past him with her nose in the air. Yes, that would be satisfying.

She lay back on the bed, texted Lailla. At least she could talk to Lailla about what had happened with Ben. Maybe she knew something about Ben from the gossip at school. Maybe he had a girlfriend. That would explain a lot.

She sent a message to Lailla. "Ben was even weirder today than ever. That's it. I don't want to see him anymore. He is just too strange." But there was no answer.

She lay on her bed, staring at her reflection in the dark window, thinking about the day and the conversation with Victoria.

Three weeks to wait and train.

Wouldn't it be amazing if Victoria would let her try riding Sand in the clinic? Kuna was a good horse but Sand was the horse she really needed if she was going to continue to compete. He was taller, better built for dressage and well-trained as well.

Perhaps this new teacher who was coming would help her persuade Victoria to let her give Sand a try.

She swung her legs over the side of the bed, limped over to her computer, opened her email, and this time she typed in Victoria's address.

"I've been thinking a lot about Sand," she wrote. "I have found some more books and material about retraining horses that have been traumatized."

She stared at the email. She thought about the story Victoria had told her, of Sand on the highway at night, of a big truck bearing down on him. He must have been so terrified. And then months of vet care and standing in his stall while his hoof grew out and his leg strengthened. Yet whenever Willy took him for a walk, he seemed calm and relaxed. Willy had a picture of Sand that Victoria had sent her. It showed Sand doing a collected canter pirouette. Wow, he must have been wonderful to ride, she thought.

Victoria had ridden him a few times in the ring, and he had stayed calm so far. Victoria had told Willy that perhaps when he was over his scare, Willy would be able to ride him but she also said she still didn't trust him. "A horse that has been that traumatized can always surprise you," she said. "I'm not ready to relax with him yet."

"Awright, Sand," Willy muttered. The picture in her mind had made her ashamed. Five minutes ago, she had been ready to give up her life and sit in her room and sulk forever. Just because some dude she didn't even care about had been rude.

She opened up chat to see if Lailla was there. She was.

"Did you get my text?" Willy typed. "Ben called and offered to drive me to riding and then he was a total jerk. That friendship is so over."

"He has really been acting strange," Lailla wrote back. "Just got kicked out of school, or so I heard. Big policeman daddy-man not happy."

"Really . . . why?"

"Rumour is he brought a toy gun to school — one of these replica things. He told someone it was a joke but Principal McKay didn't see it that way. Trust me, you're better off without him around. He's gone majorly weird."

"That is so dumb . . . a gun in school. Really? What did he think would happen?"

"Yep, messed up is what he is. Doing some major drugs. Or so I hear. So what else is new?"

"This amazing riding teacher is coming," Willy wrote back. "Why don't you come over here? Then we can talk."

"Yes! On my way, soon as I get this dumb math homework off my desk. I'll be there in an hour. You have any frozen pizza?"

■

Her days were full of swimming, riding, physio, plus hanging out with Lailla after school. She started working harder at her neglected schoolwork. Doing her classes by correspondence was boring but having Lailla around to talk to helped. She thought often about Ben but he seemed to have disappeared entirely from school and from the town.

Victoria was clearly disappointed. She asked Willy a couple of times if she had seen Ben.

Willy explained that he had said he had other things to do. She didn't want to talk about Ben.

One morning over breakfast, Willy's mom said, "Willy, I

hope you don't mind. I am going to start volunteering at the animal shelter two afternoons a week walking the dogs. I am thinking I might foster one of their dogs until it can find a home. What do you think?"

"Yes, yes, yes," Emily said. "I want a dog, I've always wanted a dog, oh Mom, bring a little puppy home, a little white fluffy puppy. Yes, yes, yes." She jumped up from the table and ran upstairs screaming, "Doggie, here doggie, doggie, doggie."

"Goodness. We'll have to see," her mom said. But she was smiling when she said it, and when she left the house that afternoon she was humming under her breath. The house felt lighter when she was gone. Willy liked being alone, liked the sense of responsibility. She did homework for a while and then wandered out to the kitchen, made herself a sandwich, and went back to work. What she had left to finish was math homework, her least favourite subject. She shouldn't have left it for last. She tried, she told herself. She truly tried. She just didn't get math. She needed help. A nice handsome young math tutor would be good about now.

She got up again and limped to the living room window. She was trying to walk without the canes but she only did it in the house where no one could see her and the carpet would cushion her if she fell. She had to exaggerate the roll of her hips from side to side to make her legs move. Now she made it to the big picture window and looked out the driveway. It was such a gorgeous day, mid September, and the blossoms on the overgrown rambling rose bush were still out.

The leaves were just starting to change but the roses continued to scent the air.

She used to have a tire swing on their big maple tree when she was little. Maybe she should just go outside and lie in the late afternoon sun — try to maintain her summer suntan.

And then she saw a familiar car across the street, parked among the other cars. Except there weren't many cars on their quiet residential tree-lined street during the day. Almost everyone was at work. Or should be. But that silver Honda looked like Ben's car — well, the car he drove around in. She assumed it was his dad's car. But why would it be sitting on her street? True, there were lots of silver Hondas in town. Although no one on this block had one. Most of the men drove trucks; most of the women with kids drove mini-vans. They were a boring bunch that way. Predictable.

She looked more closely. It looked as if someone were sitting in the car, slumped down so they couldn't be seen. She needed a closer look but she didn't want to go limping across the street to find some perfect stranger catnapping in his car. She got her canes, went to the back of the house, where the dining room had glass sliding doors that led out to the garden. There was a stone-flagged patio out there; she had to be careful that, as she slid her feet over the stones, she didn't trip on the sharp edges. She made it over the patio and onto the grass. She went down the side of the house to the gate that led into the front yard. She stopped. She was almost sure it was Ben.

And then abruptly, the figure straightened up, the car started and whoever it was drove away.

"You're fantasizing," Willy said out loud. She went back into the house but now she couldn't settle down to work. She was restless and, for once, full of energy. Her legs twitched and jumped. She wanted to go out, walk, play. The sun called her, it was just too bright to stay in. She went back outside and sat down in one of the patio chairs. No doubt about it. She was bored. She wanted friends. She wanted to visit, to dance, to party, to play. She sighed, put her head in her hands. Was this what the future offered? Loneliness? Boredom? Sitting by herself in an empty house?

No. Time to kick that sad old fantasy in the butt. There had to be more for her.

She went back in the house and phoned Lailla but only got her voicemail. Of course, she was still at school. Back outside. She was tired of feeling helpless, restless. What did she really want to do? She wanted to go to the stables, hang out with Sand, help Victoria. She was strong enough now to do chores, to do grooming, even to clean feet, as long as she had her canes nearby and didn't move too fast.

When her mom came home, she'd talk with her about spending some more time at the stables, volunteer one or two afternoons a week. There was always lots to do around the stables, and she wanted to start working more with Sand. She could ride him, she was sure. She just had to talk Victoria into it. And Victoria would be glad for the help. From listening to her, Willy had figured out that Victoria ran the stables on a series of grants, on the student fees, with help from a small army of devoted volunteers and a tiny salary for herself.

That afternoon, her mom came home bringing not one but two fluffy white puppies, tiny nippy bundles of energy. "They're not staying," her mom warned them all. "We're a foster family until they get homes."

Yeah, right, Willy thought to herself.

Em was beside herself with joy. She shrieked when she saw the puppies. They immediately began gnawing on her shoelaces. Her mom had bought a red rubber ball and Emily took the puppies outside and threw the ball for them until supper was ready.

Willy texted Lailla after supper. "I thought I saw Ben outside my house today," she typed. "Was he at school? Am I hallucinating now?"

"He wasn't at school that I saw," Lailla typed back. "Hey, please, please, please, shameless begging here. When are you coming back? It's soooooo lonely without you."

"Okay, will think about it," Willy wrote and then thought, hey, was that true? She had been dead set on not going to school but it was lonely at home. "Maybe after Christmas."

"What about this fall? Let's do some stuff together. Homework is fine but it is not exactly fun."

"I'm riding a lot," Willy wrote back. "Getting ready with Victoria for a competition. Plus I am going in a clinic with a coach who used to be in a wheelchair like me, and now she walks and rides and teaches riding. I am so totally stoked. And we're having a little show at the Centre in the middle of October. Wanna come?"

"Sure. So cool about riding. You sound so great. You sound like you. I'm sorry I can't share it with you. By the way, who was that other person?"

"Some sad cripple . . . I think she left town. Maybe."

"About time too."

"See you tomorrow after school?"

"Yes, see you then."

Lailla was waiting for her the next day when Willy returned home from riding, and they sat in the kitchen, drinking hot chocolate, eating cookies and playing with the two new puppies, now temporarily named Fats and Tootles.

"Rumour is that Ben left town after the gun thing. I think his dad was so embarrassed he sent him off somewhere. Can't be a cop in a small town with a kid with a gun fetish."

"But he was so nice," Willy said.

"Nice and crazy. Maybe he went to be with his mother."

"He said she died when he was little."

"Wow, sad."

"Guess that is that then. End of a brief era. Maybe he just felt sorry for me."

"Rumour around school is that he took some bad drugs, some of those crazy-making drugs, and he's never been the same."

"That is so dumb."

"Maybe he was just lonely. Or emotionally screwed up. Imagine growing up in a whole bunch of small towns with a cop for a dad and no mom. Now that's weird."

"I wonder what his dad is like?"

"He's a cop. Probably got lots of rules. Cops are cops, aren't they? Sort of like robots?"

That night in bed, Willy couldn't sleep. What was it with Ben? When had he changed? Everything had been good and then the day she had walked by herself out of the arena, something had shifted. He had been so angry on the way home. Was that it? He only wanted her for a friend if she was crippled and helpless? And then to disappear without a word? What a total jerk. Was it worth it to even think about him? Or maybe Lailla was right, and there was something else going on, something she didn't understand. Drugs? Whoa. She really didn't want to get mixed up with anyone who did that stuff. But then he had a cop for a dad. So if Ben got caught, would his dad throw him in jail or try to get him off? Who could Ben turn to? Maybe he had friends he had never mentioned.

She got out of bed, turned on her computer. She didn't even know where he lived but he had to be somewhere in this small town. He had found her easily enough. She had never contacted him. He had always phoned or just showed up or sent an email.

"Not fair, dude," she muttered. "You can't just disappear." She hesitated. Should she send him an email? What could she say? Had he just dumped her as a bad idea, grown tired of her, or was something else going on? Had he really been kicked out of school? Maybe she should call him? Did she even want to talk to him? This afternoon, she had never wanted to see him again. But if he was in trouble, she couldn't just abandon him.

No, an email was easier . . . calm, impersonal. They had exchanged emails a few times about lunches and ride times. She stared at her computer. What to say?

Finally, she wrote, "Hey Ben, miss you. I'm here if you ever want to talk or hang out. If not, no big deal."

The next day, she got her mother to drive her to the stables. It wasn't her usual day. Elizabeth was busy and Victoria was nowhere around.

"Hey, Elizabeth, I am just going to take Sand out for some grass," she called. Elizabeth looked up and nodded. Willy took Sand out of his stall, put him on a longe line so he could graze and took him out to the large field at the back of the stables. But as they were passing a pile of hay bales at the back of the barn, the blue tarp over the bales crackled in the wind and Sand pulled back, yanking the rope out of Willy's hands. She staggered and then fell.

"Willy, are you okay?" Victoria called. She had been at the back of the barn. She ran towards Willy as fast as she could. Elizabeth hurried after her, and they both bent over Willy, who was still crumpled on the ground.

Several other people ran into the field, trying to stop the

horse who was running around the field from one corner to another. Sand finally ran into a corner and stopped, stood there quivering while Sharlene slid very quietly and carefully up to his head, and grabbed his halter.

Elizabeth and Victoria helped Willy back on her feet. But once she was standing, she felt dizzy and fell backwards into Victoria's strong arms.

"It's okay, I've got you," Victoria said.

She helped a shaken Willy stumble from the field and into a chair. Her legs felt like jelly.

Victoria came and knelt beside her. "Are you okay?"

"Yes, fine. What happened?"

"He spooked. After the truck accident, almost anything would spook him, but he's been fine lately. I am so sorry, Willy. It was that tarp at the end of the barn. I don't think you should work with him anymore."

"Yes, of course I can!" Willy was shocked. "He just caught me by surprise."

"Sorry, Willy, it's just not safe. I don't know what to do with him. He's not safe for any rider if he is going to behave like this. He didn't just spook. He took off and then went a bit crazy."

"It was just the tarp. He didn't mean it. What will happen to him if you don't keep him?"

"We'll try to find him another home where someone can handle him."

"But nobody will take him if they know he spooks like

that. Don't let anyone kill him." She started to cry. Big tears were running down her face.

"I don't know, Willy. We can only try. Maybe someone will take him on. Lots of horses spook but they don't usually bolt like that. He needs a strong handler. Or maybe he can go to a rescue organization somewhere."

"No, please. Keep him here," Willy said. "I can keep working with him. You can give him another chance. It wasn't his fault. Any horse would spook at that tarp."

"Willy, if you were an ordinary person, maybe. But I can't take a chance on you being re-injured. Let's not argue about it right now. You calm down and let's get Sand cooled out and put away. He's probably even more upset than you."

Willy struggled out of the chair, limped over to where Sand was now being walked up and down the row of stalls by Sharlene. When she came up to him, he stopped and put his nose down to her hands, shoved his head into her chest as if he could hide there, while she scratched behind his ears and along his chest. He was covered with sweat. She wiped her face on her sleeve and wrapped her arms around his wet neck.

"Oh, beautiful boy," she whispered. "I know you didn't mean it. You were just scared. It's okay. You were hurt. But you're getting over it."

Willy cleaned the tack while Sharlene finished walking Sand until he was cooled down. Then she helped clean him up and put him in his stall.

"Can you come tomorrow and ride Kuna?" Victoria asked. "I'll have to do some juggling of the schedule but I want to do some extra practice and the clinic starts at nine Saturday. You're riding at ten but be here at nine to start your preparation, okay?"

"Victoria, I just know one day I am going to ride Sand. I am really starting to get connected to him. He listens to me, and he tries so hard to get it right."

Victoria sighed. "Not in my stable you're not. Tomorrow at nine."

"Yes, ma'am."

When Willy got home, she opened her computer. Nothing from Ben. An email from Lailla. "Got to talk."

She opened up the chat and Lailla was waiting. "Bad day," she typed. "Got called names. Can't stand this school, this town, these people. It all sucks. Please come back to school. We can be bullied together."

"Bad day here as well. It all sucks. Come over."

"Five minutes."

Lailla was true to her word. In only a few minutes, the doorbell rang. Willy's mother answered the door as Willy limped out of her room. Lailla's dark eyes were red; tears still sparkled on her eyelashes.

"What happened?" Willy asked.

"Cassia thought the guy she likes was after me. She and her friends started giggling whenever I walked by. They'd say things like, 'oh, do you smell curry?' Or, 'my, isn't it getting dark in here?' They are so horrible."

"Why didn't you report them?"

"And say what? It's their word against mine. And there's three of them. Oh, Willy, please, please, come back to school. They used to be so scared of you. If you'd been there, they would have run away like the bunnies they are."

"Yeah, maybe."

"Really, you mean it?"

"Maybe means maybe."

"Maybe with you means probably, yes!" Lailla said.

She leaned forward, gave Willy a hug. They drank tea, ate cookies with Willy's mom, listened to music for a while and then Lailla had to go home.

Which still didn't solve the mystery of Ben. Her mind wouldn't let it go; he had been so nice. Why had he turned away like that? What had she done? It was too confusing.

And then the computer made the small beep it had when a message showed up. She checked her email. A message from Ben. Finally. She opened it.

"Sorry, sorry, sorry, sorry, I'm so stupid. But you don't need me anymore anyways. Your friend, Ben."

This was such a bizarre and confusing response that she read it over twice more. What did that mean, that she didn't need him? Was this his way of telling her to go away? But then why all the sorrys? And it ended with "your friend."

She started to reply, then hesitated. Finally she wrote, "Can we talk?" and pushed send. The phone rang a few minutes later. Her mother came to the door of her room, phone in hand and a puzzled look on her face. "It's Ben," she said, "but he sounds strange."

Willy took the phone. "Hey Ben," she said.

"Hey Willy," his voice almost whispering.

"Are you okay?"

There was a long pause. Then he said, "Sure, I'm fine. Fine. Peachy keen. As in really fine. Why do you ask?"

"You sound so strange."

He sighed. "Yeah, I'm kind of having a hard time."

"Did you quit school?"

"Can't handle it right now."

"And you quit riding? Why? You were such a good rider. You said it was good for you. We were going to be in our first horse show together. Remember? We had plans. We were going to take the para-equestrian riding world by storm?"

"Yeah. Well, yeah, sorry about that. It used to be fun but I'm past that now."

"Past it? So what are you doing?"

"Hiding," he said. "I'm hiding in my room. I quit everything."

"What are you hiding from?"

"I can't tell you, it's not safe."

"Can I come over and see you?"

"No . . . I don't know, maybe. I'll call you. I can't talk right now. It's . . . it's not safe."

The phone clicked in her ear. Willy took the phone out to

the kitchen and hung it up. She went back to her room, sat in front of the computer and thought about what to do. She sighed. She really had no idea how to deal with this phone call.

She went back out of her room, down the hall and into the kitchen. Her mom was there, mixing up a dinner casserole. She looked at Willy.

"Baby, what is wrong? Look at your face. You're white as a sheet. Did you hurt yourself?"

Willy hesitated.

"It's Ben, isn't it," her mom said. "He sounded so strange on the phone. What's going on, Willy? I wondered why he disappeared so suddenly. And you never said anything. I knew something was wrong."

Her mom sat down at the small wooden kitchen table.

Willy sighed. "I don't know what to do. But yeah, something is so wrong with Ben. That was the weirdest phone call I have ever had."

They sat at the kitchen table together and Willy laid it all out, how Ben had changed. The crazy car ride. The strange email. The weird phone conversation.

Her mother looked very thoughtful. "I would guess," she said very slowly, "that he might be dealing with some kind of emotional issue. Teenagers go through lots of hard stuff and he has moved around so much. And no mom in the picture. Maybe it's just too much for him right now. But I'm no expert."

"You mean he's gone crazy?"

Her mom sighed. "No, I am not saying that. But I agree that something seems very wrong, and he probably needs help. He at least needs to talk to someone. Maybe he's just dealing with something about being a teenage boy. Hard to say and I don't want to jump to conclusions. Do you know his dad?"

"I know he's a cop. I've seen him around."

"Hmm, I wonder if anyone knows him. Then maybe we can at least ask a question or two without sounding like nosy buttinskis. I could ask the teachers I know from the high school. See if anyone else has noticed anything. You'd think his dad would be upset if Ben has dropped out of school."

"Maybe he doesn't know."

"What do you mean?"

"Lots of kids do it. You go to homeroom, sign in, then walk out again. No one knows you're not in school except the other kids. The teachers don't notice."

"Really?"

"Jeez, Mom, where have you been?"

"I've been teaching school, remember? I know all about skipping out. But of course none of the kids I deal with would do such a thing: they are mostly so sweet."

"Hah, that's what you think."

Her mom laughed, then she stopped. Her eyes suddenly filled. "Willy," she said. "I think this is the first real conversation we've had since your accident. I've missed you so much. We used to talk all the time and then you just somehow . . . I don't know, you disappeared into yourself and I didn't know how to reach you."

"I didn't want you to reach me. What was there to say? I was this crippled kid with no future I could see."

"So what's changed?"

Willy paused. Then she said, "Walking. Riding. Plus Ben helped me a lot just by being a friend. Hanging out with him."

"Well, welcome back, sugar. And I understand. I had a lot of stuff to deal with too. You know, I used to think I was so lucky. I had the perfect family, a nice life in a small town. Yeah, I know some people might think it's boring, but it's just what I wanted. And then you got hurt. I think it shattered all of us. Especially your dad."

"I'm thinking I might go back to school after Christmas. Or even sooner. Some kids are picking on Lailla without me there to have her back. Plus I miss her. I finally figured out it's lonely hanging out with just myself."

"I think that's a very good idea."

They were both silent. Then hesitantly, Willy said, "Something else I wanted to talk to you about. There's this horse at the Therapeutic Riding Centre. His name is Sand. He was hurt in an accident, too. For a while, they weren't sure he would make it. He had to stand in a stall until his hoof re-grew. He's a great horse and then every once in a while, he just freaks out. Does something stupid. Victoria took him as a rescue horse and now she thinks they will have to get rid of him. Probably no one will take him. But I can work with him. I understand him. He trusts me. I feel like there is this bond between us. I know it sounds sappy. But sometimes you just get this connection to a horse. It's a real thing."

"What does Victoria say?"

"She won't let me ride him. He spooked at the tarp on the hay when I was walking him and then he bolted into the field. Now she doesn't even want me to work with him any more. Says it's not safe."

"Then you have to listen to her, Willy. You can't take a chance on getting hurt again."

"But if she doesn't keep him, what will happen to him?"

"I don't know."

"But he's a great horse. When he's not scared, he's fantastic to be around. I want to ride him."

"You have to listen to Victoria. You have to trust her judgment."

Willy sighed. "Mom, will you come watch me ride this weekend? This coach who is coming used to be in a wheelchair too. And Victoria is going to videotape my dressage test in October and then send it in to the national therapeutic riding competition."

"Yes, of course. Oh Willy, I am so glad you asked me to come. I am so excited about your riding. Of course I want to watch you. I want to help if I can. I wouldn't miss this for anything."

Chapter 10

"HI WILLY," SAID THE soft-voiced young woman, "my name is Judy Makine. I understand you were in a wheelchair not that long ago."

"Yes," said Willy, "but riding has helped me walk."

"Yes, me too. And physio and swimming and sheer determination. So this morning, we are going to practise some riding exercises that might be new to you. We'll start off slow and then move up to some cantering. How are you feeling?"

"Okay."

"Nervous?"

"Yes."

"Well, that's okay, we'll soon be old friends. Okay, move out on the left rein, at a working trot."

Judy sent Willy and Kuna through a series of exercises. Soon she had them working in small circles and figure eights. Then she had them working in exercises that were new to Willy and very complicated, but she and Kuna managed to do them fairly well.

At the end of the ride, Willy slid off Kuna, tired but secretly pleased with herself. She started to lead Kuna from the ring but Judy said, "Hey, wait a moment, let's have a little chat before the next group comes in. So I understand you are going to be riding in the national para-equestrian competition?"

"Yes, Victoria is going to videotape my ride next week."

"Yes, you are quite an amazing rider, given your accident. Have you ever thought of trying out for a para-equestrian team, or competing on a provincial level or even a national level? You could then think about trying out for the Canadian national para-equestrian team eventually."

"Really? Wow."

"Just keep it in mind. We are always looking for riders like you. You would need a better horse, something quite a bit bigger and trained for dressage, but I think you could do very well. It can be very expensive of course, and finding the right horse might take a while. But it is something to think about, if you are interested. You can maybe talk to your parents about it. It needs a lot of support from the whole family."

"Wow, thanks so much."

"Okay, great to meet you and Kuna here. See you tomorrow morning."

Willy left the ring with her head and her heart buzzing with excitement. Canadian para-equestrian team. What was that? Something to do with the Olympics? Like the Paralympics? Could she really go to the Olympics? What if she could ride Sand? Maybe he could be her dressage horse. She would ask Victoria about it.

But that conversation didn't go so well.

"I think it is time for me to try to ride Sand," Willy said to Victoria the next morning. She had arrived especially early so they could have this conversation. She tried to brace her shoulders to keep her voice from shaking. "I could try this morning while Judy is here. She says I need a better dressage horse. Sand could be that horse. I could just try him. He won't do anything while everyone is there and we're in the ring."

"No way. If you ride him, it won't be in my stable. I simply can't let you take that chance."

"But he tries so hard for me when I am with him, walking him around. He really listens. He trusts me. I know he does."

"I know you think that, Willy. And then when you least expect it, he is going to do something dumb, bolt for the gate or dump his rider. Someone is going to get hurt, I get sued, and that is the end of my stable."

"I can train him, I know I can. We have this real connection. I can't explain it. I just know it's there."

"Look Willy, I can't afford to keep a horse here that can't be trusted and can't earn his keep. I'll do my best to find him a good home, one where he will be safe and cared for. In the meantime, if you want to keep working with him on the ground, you can but only when Elizabeth is there to help. Any horse will spook at a tarp but he didn't just spook. He took off. He bolted. He went around that field ten times. So, no riding."

Willy turned her head away, fighting to hide her tears. She sighed and limped away to fetch Kuna from his stall and saddle him. It had taken her a while to figure out how to lead a horse and saddle him, and manage it all with only one cane instead of two. Soon, she might be able to get rid of the canes completely, and then she would walk in the door of her high school, with her head held high.

Before she reached Kuna's stall, she stopped to say hello to Sand. He pushed his head into her chest and she scratched his ears and neck. She could feel the connection with him in a way that she had never felt with any other horse. It was weird. She knew he wouldn't deliberately hurt her — that even when he was crazy with fear, he would try to protect her — but she didn't know how she knew and there was no way to explain it to Victoria. But Victoria was right. He was big and if he bolted, there was nothing she could do. If she fell off, she could be badly injured. So maybe it was nonsense. Maybe she was just sympathizing with Sand because they were both injured, and not just in their body but in other ways as well.

She leaned her head against Sand and he leaned his head into her chest and gave a long sigh. "Gotta go, pal," she said. "I'll be back later."

That morning's ride with Kuna went well. Even Willy had to admit that. He was such an earnest hard-working horse. Whatever she asked of him, he tried to do. Judy made them repeat the patterns they had done the day before. They went sideways across the arena at a trot. Judy made Willy repeat everything until she did it absolutely correctly.

Finally, they rode the correct pattern for their upcoming dressage twice without mistakes. She could see the happy glint in Victoria's eyes when she slid off Kuna and led him out of the ring. Judy was smiling at her. Her mom was waiting for her, trying not to look too excited. After the weekend riding clinic, her mom had started watching her ride and was even reading a book on dressage. "Honey, that was amazing," her mom said. "You have come so far and I am just so proud of you."

"Next Wednesday," Victoria announced, "we will video-tape your riding and send it in to the national contest. You will get to ride the dressage test twice so if you and Kuna blow it the first time, you will get a second chance. But I don't think you will. You are riding very well. Wear your riding coat, white breeches, polish your boots, look spiffy. Braid your hair. We'll braid Kuna's mane and tail and polish his toes too."

Willy and her mom chatted on the way home from the clinic, about homework and Willy's mom volunteering at the animal shelter. "You should come with me, Willy," her mom said. "We just got in a whole litter of puppies someone had abandoned. They were found in a garbage bag in an alley.

Just imagine. What kind of person would do such a thing? But they are doing fine now. We had to bottle feed them at first but now they are on solid food. So cute. Some kind of Rottweiler cross most likely. It's so hard to find homes for all the dogs and cats we have."

Willy didn't answer. She stared out the window and then she turned to look at her mother. "Why can't we buy Sand? He's like those dogs at the shelter. He's been mistreated and now he needs a good home. We could board him at the stable and I could work with him really slowly, until he felt safe. And Victoria could help me. If we worked him on a longe line in a round pen at first, he wouldn't be able to do anything. He couldn't spook or bolt. And then maybe he could be my dressage horse."

"Buy him? Willy, we've been through this, remember. Victoria has forbidden you to ride him. What are you talking about?"

"Mom, you told me once that you would do anything to help me get well."

"Yes, of course I would."

"This is going to sound dumb."

"What is?"

"It's just that . . ." Willy hesitated.

"Yes?"

"It's just when I'm around him, I feel as if there's some connection. He trusts me somehow. Maybe he knows we both are hurt. I don't know. It's weird. It just feels as if he is my horse."

"Hmm."

Willy took a deep breath. "Mom, Victoria is wrong about this. She's my teacher and I think she is the greatest. She has taught me so much and I do respect her. But she's just wrong. She just is. Somehow I have to prove to her that Sand can be my horse. He's a great horse. She just doesn't see that. She got this idea that he's dangerous, and I think she's wrong because I am the one he trusts."

"Willy, Victoria is far more experienced than you."

"I know."

"She knows way more about horses and training than you do."

"I know. And she's wrong about this." There was silence in the car. "Mom, I've been around him. I know him, way better than Victoria does. Please listen to me. I have been doing so much reading about doing training and therapy with horses. I have so many ideas. I think I can help him. I would go on working with him like I've been doing. Take him for walks. Longe him. Take him right back to basics and retrain him slowly until he feels safe with me. He bolts out of fear. It would be therapy for both of us. He's my horse and I want to keep working with him. I have been working with him. A lot."

"Willy, he is a beautiful horse. And you do need a new dressage horse. He would be the perfect horse for you if he were safe."

"So you might think about it?"

"No, absolutely not. If Victoria says no, then the answer is no."

"Mom, you are not listening to me."

"Yes, I am, but my first concern is your safety and for the stables, not some romantic idea about saving a horse from himself. Forget it."

Willy was furious as she limped into her room. No one was listening to her. They all thought she was making up her ideas about Sand, but she knew she was right.

She was also absolutely exhausted. She had worked so hard in riding today — harder than usual because Judy had demanded so much from her. She had managed to do it. Now she slumped into a chair, slid off her breeches and socks, rubbed her aching muscles.

Her legs were definitely getting stronger. Kuna had responded really well because she was able to be much clearer in the signals she gave him. All she wanted now was a long shower, maybe a chat with her sister, and a big dinner and sleep. And some plan to change Victoria's and thus her mother's mind about Sand. She had to talk to Lailla about it.

But first, automatically, she turned on her computer to check her email.

And there it was, another email from Ben.

"Dear Willy: I am going away for a while. I have to get away. I know you don't want to talk to me anymore even though you said you did, but I am glad we were together — for a little while anyway. I really miss you. Bye."

Willy sat back. This was even weirder than his last email.

He missed her but he was going away? Where? Why? What was going on? She picked up her cell phone, dialled his number. It went straight to voicemail. She tried it again. This time it rang and rang. Finally a tinny voice said, "The cellular customer you are calling is away from the phone and not responding at this time."

She picked up her phone again and texted Lailla. "Lailla, can you come over?"

"Not right now. Sunday night dinner with my folks. Why? What's up?"

"Gotta tell you about it. Not on the phone."

"Sorry, also grounded for fighting."

"What!?"

"Long story. You know who went after me again on Friday. This time I yelled at them and now I am the one in trouble. Parents giving me evil looks. Principal Hooey lectured. Blah blah. Everyone upset. The gossip girls are buzzing."

"Oh, no, so so so sorry. Can I come over there?"

"No, grounded is grounded. TTYL."

Now what could she do? She had no way to get to Ben's house but perhaps his dad had an actual phone number in the phone book, one she could look up. What the heck was Ben's last name? Right. It was on his Facebook page. Ben Morris.

There were two Morrises in the phone book. She tried the first one. Voicemail. "You have reached Lisa and Larry Morris." Nope. He was a single dad. She punched in the second number. "Hi, you have reached Joe Morris. I am not in right now. Please leave a message."

"Hi, Mr. Morris. I'm a friend of Ben's. My name is Willa. I am trying to reach him. Can you tell him to give me a call on my cell?" and very slowly she repeated the ten-digit number. "Thanks."

Now what to do? She looked at the address again. Not that far but too far to walk.

Hmm. What if she called the police station? What could she say? Hi, I'm worried about your weird kid sending me weird emails. Nope, that wouldn't do. He says he's leaving. Yes, that sounded scary.

Ask her mom to drive her over there? No, wrong time and place — it wouldn't do. Her mom was in the kitchen making dinner. Willy could hear her chopping something and then the thin smell of onions wafted through the door. And then garlic frying.

Bicycle? Could she even ride a bicycle anymore? She hadn't been on a bike since the accident. As far as she knew, her bike was still in the garage. Or maybe her sister rode it. She decided at least to go and look. Her mom was busy, would be in the kitchen for a while from the sounds and smells.

Willy limped soundlessly down the hall on the carpet, out the sliding glass doors, across the deck. The grass was freezing on her bare feet. The side door to the garage was open. Wow, she hadn't been in here for a long time. Funny how garages accumulated so much junk. And there was her bike, covered with dust, hanging on the back wall. She went back in the house, slid on her shoes, back outside, through and out of the garage, through the back gate into the alley. She wandered down the alley, using one cane, slowly and carefully. She hadn't been here for so long either. It was cold and getting dark. She came out to the street, looked up and down at the familiar cars and yards. She had lived here her whole life. She knew everyone on this street. Once it was the safest place in the world and then, after the car accident, nothing and nowhere had seemed very safe, except perhaps sitting in her wheelchair in her room. Riding in cars was especially difficult but she had gradually got used to it.

She went slowly down the sidewalk with her cane. This was the first time she had done more than walk from the car to her house and from the house to the car, and now just see what she had missed. Newly painted doors, a new fence, a dog she didn't remember barking at her from a yard that had been carefully landscaped. Had the French family sold their house? She'd have to ask her mother. And there was old Miss Emily, who must be over ninety, peering suspiciously at Willy from behind her prize rose bushes now bare of leaves.

"Willy, is that you? Nice to see you out and about, dear."

"Nice to see you too, Miss Emily." Willy had always wondered why she was called Miss Emily when everyone else seemed to have real names but that was just what she was called.

"And how is your dear mother?"

"Oh, she's fine."

"That's nice, dear, say hello for me." And Miss Emily went back to pruning her roses as if it were a perfectly ordinary thing that Willy should be stumping along with a cane. She made it back to her own yard thinking about how Miss Emily walked, bent over, and how crooked her hands were. Willy walked up the driveway and around to the back deck. She hadn't solved the problem of Ben but she had figured out something about herself, that she could walk out in the evening sun and look at people's yards and not feel self-conscious about her cane and her wobbly walk.

She went back to her room, tried Ben's cell phone again, left another message. Tried again to text Lailla. No one was answering.

Her mom called her. "Supper's almost ready, Willy. Your dad called. He's going to be late. Some meeting or other and your sister is over with her friend Janet. So it's just you and me, kiddo."

Willy sat at the table, toying with her food. It was one of her favourite casseroles; she could tell her mom had gone to a lot of effort, but she was thinking about Ben. Finally, she said, "Do you think after supper, you could run me over to Ben's house? He sent me another email. I think I really need to go talk to him."

"Do you think that's a good idea?"

"Maybe if I see him, I can talk some sense into his head."

"Do you know where he lives? Do you want me to wait for you?"

"I have an address. If he's there, he can run me home."

"Didn't you phone him?"

"Yeah, he's not answering."

"If he's not there, we're coming straight home."

"Yeah, of course."

"So what did he say in this email?"

"Just . . . that he was having trouble, that he might be going away. He said he missed me."

Her mom gave her a long level glance. She had always been able to tell when Willy was lying or at least, leaving something out. Or at least she always said she could.

They stacked the dishes in the dishwasher, got in the van and drove to the address that Willy had copied out of the phone book. The silver Honda that Ben usually drove was in the driveway. Did that mean Ben was at home? Or that his dad was home? It was dark now but street lights illuminated the yard.

Willy clambered out of the van and rang the doorbell; no one answered. She turned her hands palms up to her mom's inquiring glance out the car window and then limped around to the back of the house. There were glass doors at the back and a tiny deck with a roof. The grass was long and untended. The flower beds were full of weeds. Dead vines spiralled up the posts holding up the deck roof. There was a garage at the back. Willy peered in the glass doors, couldn't see anything, then limped to the open side door of the garage. Nothing inside but piles of junk, cardboard boxes, a broken bicycle lying on the floor.

She turned around to go back. The sun was just setting. The shadows were long over the quiet street. Willy shivered.

Where would a seventeen-year-old kid run to? A big city probably — she had read about street kids. Their small town wasn't somewhere anyone could hide in for long. But why would someone who had a home and a dad do such a thing?

She got back in the van with her mom. "No one around," she said.

"Willy, just what is going on? Why are you so worried?"

Willy sighed. "In the email, Ben said something like, it had been nice to know me. It sounded so weird. It was like an email you'd send if you were going to do something crazy, like run away, or worse."

"Willy, this is serious. If he has run away, his father has to know about it."

"Yeah, you're right. I just thought maybe I could talk to him and calm him down, then I could figure out what is really going on."

"You need to talk to his dad."

"He's a cop."

"So, cops are people, dads, moms."

"But wouldn't that be like . . . ?"

"Yes?"

"Well, like tattling, like calling the cops on your friends?"

"Willy, there's a time for loyalty and then there's a time when the best thing you can do for a friend is get them some help."

"I still want to talk to him. Maybe I can help."

At that moment, an RCMP cruiser turned into the driveway. A man in a police uniform stopped the car and got out. He saw them sitting in the van and came over. Willy's mom rolled down the window.

"May I ask what you are doing here?" he asked. He stood back a little from the window and looked them over, ducked his head to look at the van and its license plate.

Before her mom could answer, Willy leaned over and said, "My name is Willa. I'm a friend of Ben's. I was hoping he'd be home."

"Ben? You're a friend of Ben's?" He frowned. "Do you go to school together?"

"No, we didn't meet at school, we met at physio. He started driving me to riding lessons. Wait."

She opened the van door, got her canes, slid out and hobbled around the side of the van. "He sent me an email. I just came to make sure he's okay."

"Why would you think he's not okay?"

"I didn't. I mean, I don't know. I mean, the email was kind of weird. I just wanted to see him, say hello?"

"When was the last time you saw him?"

"A while ago. Like, a month or more."

The man stared at her. "You haven't talked to him then?"

"Just emails."

"Come inside," he said. "Right now. Both of you. I don't know who you are. You need to tell me what you know, if you have any idea where he is." He rubbed one hand over his face and shook his head.

His phone rang. He pulled it out of his vest pocket and answered.

"No," he said. "No, he wouldn't. He didn't ... all right. I'll be right there. Don't do anything. Wait for me."

"What is it?" Willy asked.

The man looked at her as if he had never seen her before. Then he shook himself. "Go home." he said. "Right now. I've got to go. I'll call you. Later."

He ran to his police cruiser, jumped in, started the motor, backed out of the driveway and took off, siren wailing.

"He can't call me," Willy said. "He won't know my number unless he's checked his messages."

"He's a cop, sweetie. He'll find you ... if he remembers. If he even knows who you are. He didn't even ask. I wonder what is going on? I hope Ben is okay."

"Me too. How can we find out?" Willy's voice came out too loud, too high-pitched.

"Honey, it is really none of our business. We should go home and just wait until we hear something or you hear from Ben. Or maybe we should just drop it."

"Mom, Ben is my friend. And he sent me that strange email. I am so worried. I want to find out right now. I think I have a right to know something."

"Yes, I confess I'm a little worried as well."

"What about your friend who works for the newspaper? Don't reporters usually know what's going on? She could find out if there has been an accident or if someone has been hurt or something like that. Couldn't she? Worth a try, anyway."

"It's late. She wouldn't be at work right now."

"But she could call someone. If there's been some trouble, she could find out about it."

"Yes, she could. Okay, hang on." Willy's mom fished a cell phone out of her purse.

"Hi, Joannie? Yeah, hi, it's Liz. Listen, sorry to bother you at home. We're looking for some information on a young guy named Ben . . ."

"Morris," Willy hissed.

"Yes, we're looking for some information about an incident possibly involving a Ben Morris. Ben M-o-r-r-i-s. Oh really. Okay. Oh no. Would you know which hospital? Okay, thanks so much, Joannie. Yes, I'll wait." There was a long pause. Willy looked out the window at the green lawn, tapping her fingers nervously on the van door.

"Yes, he's a friend of Willy's. She's concerned. Oh, the General. Right, I understand. Yes, she's doing so much better. Yes, thanks. Lunch? Sounds great. Give me a call." She clicked the phone shut and turned to face Willy.

"He's at the General. In the psych ward. Joannie called her paper. He stole a car and wrecked it. Some reporter had already checked it out."

"The psych ward? What? Mom, this is not making sense. I have to see him."

"Yes, the psych ward. And no, you can't see him. We'll just have to go home and wait for news."

Chapter 11

THE NEXT DAY, as soon as Willy got up, she phoned the General Hospital. She had been there a few times for check-ups. It was a big white building on top of a hill above the town.

"Are you his family?" asked a voice.

"No," she said. "Just a friend."

"I'm sorry, you will have to get news from the family or have them put your name on a list so you can receive news. Goodbye." The phone clicked in her ear.

Fine. She called the local RCMP office. No, Officer Morris was not there. Yes, they would pass on a message to him and her cell number. She showered, dressed, wondered what to do. She could go to the stables and work. Take Sand for a walk. Do some more training. That would pass the time. She had been spending every spare moment with him lately and it was making a difference. Victoria hadn't said anything.

Breakfast first. She used to hate breakfast. But since she decided to get well, she ate carefully, healthy cereal, milk, juice, vitamins. Her mother was sitting at the table, drinking an extra cup of coffee and playing with the puppies, one on her lap, one chewing on her slippers. She looked up and laughed when Willy came into the kitchen.

"I'm afraid I'm going to go through a lot of slippers at this rate, before these brats find a new home. It had better be soon. We're all getting too attached to them."

"Mom, what were you thinking? Of course Emily is now velcroed to them. She'll never let them go. Fostering. Right. Just adopt them. Get it over with."

"But the whole idea is to move them on and take more animals. Otherwise, these poor sweeties would be sitting in cages at the shelter. This way, they are here, playing ball and eating slippers."

"Yeah, you just had to bring home the two cutest puppies in the shelter. Why not bring some poor droopy old mutt with saggy jowls that no one is ever going to want?"

"And then have to send him back when he's had a taste of home life? How cruel is that. At least this way, these puppies are properly socialized when they move to a new home."

"Socialized," snorted Willy. "Spoiled rotten is more like it."

"Any word on Ben?"

"The hospital says they can't tell me anything because I'm not family. I called his dad but he hasn't called back."

"He will. He seemed like a nice man."

"For a cop."

"Oh, c'mon, Willy. I am sure Ben loves his dad."

"I don't know. He's never said much about him. In fact, he never talked about him at all other than to say his dad didn't know him. That was one weird thing about our friendship. I told him lots about me and he seemed interested, but whenever I asked him questions, he clammed up. So I stopped asking. All he ever said was that they moved all the time."

"Yeah, that must be tough. All those new schools, small towns, cliques, probably kids and other people giving him a hard time over his dad being a cop."

"He did say once that people liked to do drugs in front of him to see his reaction."

"Well, there's drugs everywhere. You don't have to be a cop's kid to run into that. Or to figure out how to deal with it. So what's your plan for today, honey?"

"I thought I might spend some time with Sand, trying some new stuff, but I am also thinking I will hang around here until I hear about Ben. I've got some reading to do. You know, Mom, I keep reading, trying to figure out how to get into Sand's head. It's so interesting. I keep learning new stuff about how to just hang out with horses, get them to trust people, get them to relax. I want to learn to train horses naturally. I think that is so cool. Victoria is interested too, but she doesn't have much time to read. Just keeping the stables together takes all her energy."

"I think that is fascinating, sweetie. Me too. I've been reading all kinds of stuff about training dogs. Oh no, what if I start collecting dogs? I can see it coming. We'll be on TV. One of those crazy animal-hoarder families."

"Mom, I still want us to buy Sand. I want to talk to Dad about it. Even if I never ride him, at least he would be safe and have a home."

"Willy, if you can persuade Victoria to let you keep working with him, then your dad and I might consider buying him. Actually, I did talk to your dad. We talked about it quite a bit because you said it was the one thing that would make you happy. But Victoria says it is not safe to ride him. So, safety versus happiness. That is a very tough call for us as parents. Let's talk more tonight, when your dad is home. Of course, he complained about money but that is just your dad. That's what he does. And if I go back to teaching, he won't be able to complain about that anymore. Okay, I am off to the shelter to walk some of the dogs. If you want to go to the stables, call me. See you later, sweetie, text me if there's any news, okay?"

She went to the door, slid out of her slippers, which were immediately claimed by the puppies, and slid on her jacket. Willy followed the triumphant puppies into the living room and wrestled her mom's slippers away from them. She gave them chew toys instead and then flopped onto her bed to read.

Just as she lay down, her phone rang.

"Hi Willy, this is Joe, Joe Morris, Ben's dad."

"Hey, Mr. Morris. How is Ben?"

"Ben had a little accident but he should be fine. Thanks for your interest but we'll be okay."

The phone clicked in her ear.

Willy was so surprised she simply stared at the phone. The long list of questions she had been going to ask died in her throat. She clicked off her cell phone, lay back on the bed, stared at the ceiling, thinking. Eventually she went back to her reading although it was hard to concentrate. Thoughts of Ben, frightened and possibly hurt, kept intruding.

But the material on training horses pulled her in. She began making notes and the notes turned into a report for Victoria. Totally absorbed, she was startled when her mom knocked on her door to call her for lunch. She hadn't even heard her mom come back from the animal shelter.

After lunch, her mom drove her to the stable. She limped down the hall to Victoria's office. The office door was closed. She went on past the stalls. For once, the place was quiet. The horses were out grazing and no one was having a lesson. She found Victoria at the back of the barn, in the feed room, measuring buckets of grain and beet pulp out for the evening feed.

"Victoria, can we please talk about Sand."

Victoria sighed and went on measuring. "I told you my decision."

"But I'm the one who has been working with Sand on the ground, and I think we have a real connection. I think I can ride him; I think you need to at least let us try. He's not the same horse that he was when he came here. He's learning to trust me. He's not as afraid anymore."

"And you know this how?"

"From working with him every couple of days. Mom has been driving me here. I've been spending a lot of time just being with him. I've been reading all this stuff about natural horsemanship. Elizabeth and I have been working with him to get him to trust me and follow me even without a halter and lead. You need to come and watch us, please. He's so different now."

"Okay, fine," Victoria said. "Convince me. Let's see this miracle. But if anything goes wrong, that's it."

Together they went out to the field where Sand was grazing with the other horses. He came over as soon as he saw Willy walking towards him with her cane. She slid the halter she had brought onto his head and clipped the lead onto the halter. She led Sand into the arena and began walking him around the ring. Then she unclipped the lead and Sand walked beside her without the lead. She walked, stopped, turned, went in figure eights and Sand stayed right at her shoulder. She stopped right in front of Victoria and Sand leaned his dark brown head forward to be praised and petted. Willy clipped the lead back onto his halter.

"Hmm," Victoria said. "You're right. That was impressive. When have you had time to do all this? I didn't know you were doing this."

"I do a little bit every couple of days. We're usually outside in the field so you didn't see because you were in the ring teaching. I didn't want to put pressure on him so we went slowly but he learned quickly. He is already well-trained so it was more like finding out what he already knew."

"Well, I didn't know he could do that. Okay, let's put a saddle on him and see if he stays calm under saddle."

Willy led him to the saddling area, and Victoria saddled and bridled him and then Willy led him back into the arena. She led him around again and he calmly followed her all the way around the arena, just as he had before. She led him both with the lead and without it.

"Come in and park right in front of me," Victoria called, and Willy led Sand over and they both stood at attention in front of Victoria.

"Hmm," Victoria said again. "You are right. He is a very different horse. His attitude, his behaviour, his work ethic, have all changed. I can see it in him, in his eyes and his body language. He has made a real connection with you. It's amazing. Okay. Let's give this a real try so we know what we are working with. I know I am breaking my word and changing my mind, but I have to understand what is going on here."

Victoria clipped the lead line onto the side on the bridle and led Sand over to the mounting block. "Up you go," she said to Willy. "But I am staying in control every minute."

Willy's heart was pounding. This was the moment she had been working and training and hoping for. She eased very carefully onto Sand's back. He stood perfectly still, only turning his head to check that she was now on his back instead of on the ground. The three of them went around the ring again and then Victoria clipped on a longe line.

Sand and Willy walked and trotted in circles around Victoria in both directions. Sand was quiet and well-behaved.

Finally, they stopped again in front of Victoria, and Willy loosened the reins. "Let him walk on a loose rein," Victoria said. They went around the ring in complete silence and then stopped by the gate.

"All right," Victoria said. "You are right. He is so beautiful. The two of you look wonderful together. There is no question you could both go far in the dressage world." She reached out and stroked Sand's sweaty neck and he nosed her hand. "Before he was hurt, he was a very well-trained horse, on his way to a great career. The question now is, can he go back there? Can he handle the pressure? Can the two of you go there together? You seem to truly understand each other. Okay, off, let's go talk."

They untacked Sand, cleaned him off, put him back out in the field with the other horses. Then they went back to Victoria's office. Willy got her pack and fetched the notes on horse training she had made. "This is what I have been reading," she said.

Victoria flipped through the pages, frowning. "Interesting, right, good," she said. "Yes, I think this is exactly what he needs, more of this kind of work, and now, it looks as if you could start your dressage training on him. Why not? All right, maybe, just maybe, I was wrong, Willy. Although I don't think he would be safe to take on trail rides or outside the ring. And if this works out, you can try out for the BC para-equestrian dressage team."

"My parents said if you changed your mind about him, they will buy him."

"Really?"

"Yes, and board him, so then you can afford to have him here."

"Okay, that would definitely solve a lot of problems."

"And you can stop worrying about finding him a home. His home is here."

"Okay, Willy, okay, I get it. But I am not letting you buy him yet. I am going to ride him myself for a bit and train him along with you. You can start riding him. We'll start very gradually and see how it goes. As long as you are right and he doesn't freak out again, then this will work. But it's a big risk. I might be crazy and I'm still not sure this is the right thing to do. However, riding is always risky. It's part of the game. And when I think about what a crazy terrified mess he must have been after he was injured, and what a difference you have made, yes, it's impressive. You've earned the right to try him."

That night, after supper, after Emily had scraped and rinsed the dishes and Willy had put them in the dishwasher, their mom said, "Okay, family. We all need to talk. Your dad and I have been thinking about Willy and Sand and Willy's riding career. This concerns all of us as a family because this means a big time commitment and a big money commitment. Willy has an announcement she wants to make."

"Victoria says I can ride Sand, so Mom and Dad can buy him for me. And then I can try out for the BC para-equestrian team," Willy said. "C'mon, Em, let's go outside and torture the puppies."

"Willy, sit right down," roared her dad. "This is about you, young lady. You start asking for an expensive commitment from me, you'd better be prepared to sit and listen to a lecture." But there was a smile lurking behind his frown.

Willy saw it and shrieked. "Yes, yes, yes, I can see you smiling. Yes, Daddy, thank you. Em, Daddy is smiling!"

"Wait just a minute. I haven't said what we expect from you, and it's a long list."

"Yes, Daddy, whatever you want. I'll do." Willy sat in a chair, folded her hands in front of her, prepared her face in a solemn mask.

"Well," her father began, and then frowned. "Willy, I simply can't talk to you when you are being so ridiculous."

"Ridiculous? I'm just sitting here."

"That's exactly what I mean. You're being way too good."

"But, Daddy . . ."

"Now listen. Here's the deal." His face was twitching as he tried not to smile. "Yes, your mom and I have decided to buy this horse. And yes, I did go to see him. Your mom and I had a talk with Victoria and we also talked to Judy Makine.

Victoria's an amazing woman, Willy, I am glad I met her and glad she's your teacher. She's still worried about Sand, but says you are working with him and have accomplished some kind of miracle with him. She also says she can't afford to keep him unless we are his owners. So that's a bit of a win-win for everyone. It was really Judy that talked her into it. Victoria is still worried about whether Sand is safe for you to ride."

"Dad . . ." Willy began.

"But she told us that if you can keep on with the training program you have with him — it seems to be doing you both good — then you can start training for your upcoming para-equestrian dressage test."

"Dad . . ."

"So Willy, if you are going to start training as an athlete, this means discipline, this means having a positive attitude, this means getting in shape, this means listening to what your mom tells you."

"Daaaad . . ."

"Yes, Willy?"

"It's fine, I agree to everything. Sand is my horse. I knew it as soon as I saw him. And yes, I'll be the bestest goodest kid ever. You'll see. I already had the attitude change, you just didn't notice. I'm your girl now. I'm back."

She put out her hand and her dad shook it. Then he got up and hugged her. Then Em hugged her. Her mom just smiled at them all.

Sand was hers. He was really almost hers.

She had to make even more promises, it turned out, including finally to go to counselling. But she didn't care. All of those things were easy. She wanted Sand, and she knew that he wanted her, and she knew she could make him better. And one day she would ride on the Canadian para-equestrian team.

She also needed to see Ben. She had phoned his father the next day.

"Mr. Morris, I would really like to visit Ben. I think he would really like to see me too."

"Who are you again?"

"I am a friend of Ben's. We met at therapeutic riding."

"Oh right. You were at my house asking about him."

More and more, she did not like this man. No wonder Ben was so lonely. She hadn't done anything wrong, and yet somehow this man was making her feel guilty.

"Why do you want to see him?"

"Just to visit. Hang out. See how he's doing? Everybody needs friends."

He sighed deeply.

"Yes, the doctor did say he could have visitors. But only one at a time. And only for ten minutes."

Her mom drove her to the hospital where Joe Morris was waiting in the parking lot. He nodded and said, "Nice to see you again. Willa? Was that your name? This way."

He led her into the hospital, into the elevator. They went

up five floors and to another desk where Ben's father introduced her to a nurse, who then led her down a long hall, and
past another vigilant nurse behind a desk who stared at Willy
with her cane as if she were some nasty bug. This nurse followed her down the hall and unlocked the door.

"I'll be back in ten minutes," she said.

But then Ben . . . and not Ben. The same Ben at first, her
friend, dark hair, warm smile when he stood up to greet her.
White t-shirt. Blue jeans. She hugged him, he hugged her
back. His body felt as if the bones were all sticking out.

They sat down, he on his narrow, neatly made hospital bed
with its blue cover, and she in an orange chair beside the bed
so he was higher than her and she had to look up.

"How's riding?" he said, and his smile was still the same.
But then he didn't wait for her answer but stood up and began to prowl around the room. "I miss riding," he said. "I was
good, wasn't I? I could have been really good. I should have
stayed there. But I can go riding again when I get out of here.
I'll come back and this time I'm going to compete, maybe I'll
get a better horse, Victoria just doesn't understand, I don't
want to just ride, I need to ride and win." His words tumbled
over themselves. "But maybe riding isn't my thing, maybe I
should do something else, I was thinking of asking my dad to
get me a motorcycle, I could do motorcycle racing, that
would be really fun, all that speed."

"When do you get to go home?" Willy interrupted.

"Don't know, no one will tell me anything. My dad barely
speaks to me, he's so mad. My dad just doesn't get it."

"What do you mean?"

"He doesn't get me, he doesn't care about me, he doesn't understand what I do or say. He just gets mad at me. I can't talk to him. I can't tell him anything."

It was on Willy's lips to say, "Yeah, you stole a car and wrecked it. I'll bet he's mad," but then she hesitated.

"You're not mad at me, Willy, right? Tell me you're not mad."

"No, I'm not mad, but I don't really understand what is going on with you."

But Ben wasn't listening to her. Instead he began pacing around the room. "I just need to go home and be in my own space. I hate this place. They won't let me do anything. They won't let me out even to go for a walk. I told them I'm fine. I just want to go home. I just want out this place. Walls and walls. More walls. I hate walls. My dad knows that. Why am I here?"

Then he stopped and looked at her. "You talk to them. You make them understand. I can't stay here. I need to go home. You know what I mean. You were in the hospital. You hated it. Tell them, Willy, tell them. Tell them it's the walls. I can't stay here. Please tell them."

"I will, Ben. I'll go talk to your dad as soon as I leave. Ben, can you please sit down and just talk to me. Tell me how you're feeling?"

"Why do you want to know that?" he asked. "You don't like counsellors. You told me that. Did they tell you to come in and ask me questions?"

Ben but not Ben. Some frantic version of Ben. He sat back down on the bed. He put his head in his hands and swayed back and forth and wouldn't look at her or say anything more. The nurse knocked on the door and let her out. Ben didn't say anything as she left. As she limped down the hall, her head was whirling. That wasn't the Ben she knew at all.

But it was him as well, just a lonely and confused and manic version of him. She couldn't make sense of it. Why was he talking so fast, so loud? Why was he in a locked room? What was going on? She needed to talk to someone who could explain what had happened to her friend, a friend who had made a big difference in her life, a friend she owed something to.

She went outside and sat on the hospital steps. The sun fell hot on her head and shoulders. She leaned her head in her hands. She couldn't get that last vision of Ben rocking back and forth on the bed out of her mind. He was so alone. What had happened to him that he was so alone?

When her mom parked beside the steps, Willy was relieved to get in the car, relieved to be driving away from the hospital, relieved to be going home to her dull normal life and her dull normal family.

"How was your visit?"

Willy shuddered. "It was awful. He seemed so strange. I don't get it. What is wrong with him?"

"I don't know if they have a diagnosis yet."

"But how can he just change like that?"

"I don't really know, Willy. It's pretty scary, that someone can snap like that. The brain is so mysterious. As long as everything works the way it should, then it's all fine. If it upsets you so much, perhaps you shouldn't visit him for a bit. He's got his dad and the doctors will find some medication to make him feel better."

"Of course I am going to go see him. Mom, he helped me, remember. And he just seems so alone. Maybe he needs a friend more than anything else."

"I don't know, Willy. Sometimes people in his state aren't really good to be around. They can do or say things they don't mean."

"Mom, what are you saying?"

"Sometimes people in his state can be a bit scary. He did steal a car and wreck it. He's probably going to get in a lot of trouble for that."

"All the more reason he needs a friend."

"Just be careful, Willy, okay?"

"Yeah, whatever." Willy slumped back in the seat, staring out the window. She needed someone to talk to about this. Someone who could tell her what was going on and what she could do about it all.

■

The next day was riding day. This would be her first week to begin actually riding Sand, without Victoria leading him.

She had decided as an owner-rider, she would start trying

to do her share of cleaning stalls, brushing horses, cleaning tack and all the other chores that kept the place up and running.

And she still had schoolwork online to keep up with and Lailla to talk to. But mostly now she moved and worked with a light heart. She walked with a limp but her step was light, and she was walking. That was what mattered. And she was riding.

This morning when she arrived at the stable, she led Sand out of his stall by herself and brushed him.

Victoria and Elizabeth helped her get him saddled and bridled and then led him into the ring. After Victoria clipped on the longe line and led him to the mounting block, Elizabeth helped Willy slide quietly into the saddle. Sand was fairly quiet although he skittered sideways at her weight in the saddle.

"Okay, big man," Victoria said. "Just take it easy."

After twenty minutes of doing circles and longeing, Willy felt him begin to relax. "I think that is enough for now," Victoria said. "He was pretty tense this morning. I think we should just turn him out in the field for a bit. C'mon, it's too nice a day to stay in this dusty arena. Let's go outside and go for a trail ride."

"Good idea," Willy said with delight.

She and Elizabeth turned Sand out in the paddock and then fetched Kuna from his stall. Elizabeth watched and helped a bit as Willy saddled and bridled him, and led him to where Victoria was saddling a new horse she was trying out. "I want to see how this girl behaves on the trails," Victoria said. "C'mon. We'll ride along the river."

After helping Willy onto Kuna, Victoria mounted the new horse, and they rode out through the gate at the back of the arena, down a long passage between rail fences that led onto a grassy shaded trail that ran beside the river. Occasionally, they passed people on bikes or walking dogs, but the horses behaved themselves and everything was peaceful. They kept their horses to a walk, and the new horse, named Sasha, seemed quiet and well-trained.

"We need another therapeutic riding horse," Victoria said, "and this girl seems just about perfect, so far. But I have to make sure. They have to be a certain kind of horse to work with disabled people. It's hard on the horses. They are so sensitive. They can tell when something is wrong with their rider and they try so hard to do what is wanted."

"Sand tries really hard," said Willy. "He listens to everything I tell him. He watches me."

"Of course he does. Horses really want to be part of a herd; they want to join up with people. Mostly they want to feel safe, and if the human is relaxed, they are relaxed. You have gained his trust, Willy. He feels safe with you. It is going to make you and him such incredible partners."

"People need to feel safe too," Willy said. "When I went to see Ben, it was as if there were two Bens, the normal Ben and then the one who was talking too fast and too much and didn't make a whole lot of sense, because deep down, he was really scared and didn't trust anyone."

"I am so sorry to hear that," Victoria said. "Ben was — is — a great guy. He was terrific to work with. Learned fast. Good with the horses. Sensitive and quiet. Maybe too sensitive sometimes. I hope he comes back to riding."

"He helped me a lot. Mostly by not feeling sorry for me and just doing stuff I needed. He drove me around, made me laugh, brought me here. I owe him a lot."

"Yeah, most people are scared when someone like Ben freaks out. It's the same as when a horse freaks out. The horse doesn't mean to hurt anyone. Neither did Ben."

"My mom doesn't know if I should visit him anymore but of course I should. He needs a friend."

"I would imagine Ben needs all the friends he can get. But I understand your mom's concerns. After all, he did steal a car and wreck it. He could have really hurt some people or really hurt himself."

"I don't care," said Willy. "I am going to talk to his counsellor next week."

"Thought you hated counsellors?"

"When I was really crippled, I hated the idea of counselling so much, I wouldn't go. I didn't want to listen to anyone who might talk me out of being so mad. I'm still crippled but when I ride horses, I don't feel crippled. I feel as if I can do anything. And I'm not mad at the world anymore."

"You have come a long ways," Victoria said, and laughed.

"I still remember how you looked when you first came. You scowled at everything. I remember thinking, oh-oh, here comes trouble. And boy, was I right!"

She grinned at Willy. "Here's a nice long straight stretch. Are you up for a canter?"

"Yes!"

They cantered along the wide trail. Then Victoria saw some people walking their dog in the distance and signalled to Willy to slow down. They guided their horses into a walk. The two horses walked side by side. Willy turned her face up to the warm sun. Light danced off the river.

"Ben should be here too," she said. "Not stuck in a hospital."

"Maybe the hospital is the best place for him right now."

"Maybe. But it's so gross there. Bare walls. Nothing to do. Crappy food."

"Food isn't the issue right now."

"After I got out of the hospital," Willy said, "I didn't want to talk to anyone. It felt as if I wasn't even the same person I used to be. I figured everyone would look at me and feel sorry and laugh behind my back. Poor little cripple. That's what they'd say."

"So how did it change? You're not like that now."

Willy frowned. "I didn't really even notice it changing. It's because I started doing stuff. Ben made me get out of the house, and then I came here and every time I got on a horse, I felt stronger. It was your word — capable — that made a big difference. Riding made me feel capable instead of crippled. And then I started walking. That was huge."

"Yes, you are so much stronger now."

"And then one day, I started to figure how good I had it. It was a whole lot of little things that changed me, right from the time I started riding. I went with my mom to the animal shelter one day, all those poor sad dogs and cats. And Sand being freaked the way he is. So then I started noticing that a lot of people are dealing with crappy stuff. Even my best friend Lailla, who is so cute and funny and great, she gets bullied in school 'cause her parents are from India. That is just so stupid. It makes me so mad. And now Ben."

"Yes, and now Ben."

They rode on in silence for a while.

"Well, this has been great," Victoria said, "but I've got a busy barn I'm neglecting. I'd better stop taking time off to ride and get back to shovelling horse manure. Yep, the glamorous life of a riding instructor. That's what it's all about."

They turned and trotted briskly back to the barn. By the time they reached it, Willy could feel the extra exertion in her arms, legs and back. It felt good but also painful. She was going to be glad to get home, into a hot shower, and into her comfortable desk chair. There was an English essay to write, waiting for her attention.

Her mom was waiting in the parking lot as usual. She was frowning. "Willy, I am so sorry to tell you this. There's been a development in Ben's case. He's escaped. No one knows how. He was supposed to be in a secure ward but, you know, it's a hospital. Nothing is that secure. He seemed quiet and they thought he was getting better. Now no one knows where he is."

"Oh no, Mom. What if he's hurt?"

"I think they are more worried about whether he's doing something stupid. Stealing another car. Hurting someone."

"Ben would never hurt anyone."

"Willy, he's not thinking clearly."

"But why, what is wrong with him?"

"No one really understands it, but sometimes these things happen. His mind isn't working properly. It is sending him wrong messages about what's real and what isn't. It's an accident, like your car accident, but in that case, we knew what happened and what to do to help you get better. With the mind, no one is sure."

"Will he get better?"

"Yes, Willy, he'll get better. But it might take awhile."

"Are they looking for him?"

"Of course. I would imagine his dad is frantic by now. I would be, in his shoes."

Willy's mom reached over and squeezed Willy's hand. "When I see you now, riding and strong and capable, and I remember how small and white looking you were in that hospital bed . . . And then they told us you might never walk again. Every day I give thanks. I am just so happy you're my daughter and you're alive and well."

"Mom, I have an idea where Ben might go."

"Where?"

"He loves the river. He took me down there once. I was in a wheelchair and he pushed me along the path to this one spot above the riverbank. He said there was a spot down there among the rocks that he liked so he could think and get away from everyone. He was laughing like it was all a big joke. But it wasn't."

"Hmm, why don't you call his dad and tell him?"

"Yeah, I could, I guess. But if they show up with flashing lights and cop cars, wouldn't that totally freak him out?"

"I don't know, Willy. I'm just glad it's not me dealing with it and making these decisions."

They pulled into the driveway and Willy made her slow way into the house. She shucked off her horsey sweaty clothes and climbed into the shower. Then she texted Lailla who called her immediately. Willy told Lailla about Ben and where she thought he might be.

"Well, you've got to find a way to go down there. Let's both go. We just need someone to drive us."

"Yeah, like who? Plus, it's getting dark and cold."

"Yes, you're right, Willy. It's too late right now. It will be mighty cold out there too. It's almost winter. What if Ben is out there alone? He could get hypothermia or something."

"Of course he's alone. Right now, he doesn't have any friends. Everyone is scared of him."

"Well, I would be scared too. Willy, remember what you

said about there being two Bens. The Ben you know is a nice guy. Who is this other Ben? We don't know what he might do. Maybe he doesn't know what he might do?"

"He wouldn't hurt anyone."

"You don't know that for sure."

"Right now, I don't know anything for sure. I don't know why he snapped like that, or what happened to him or what it feels like for him or what to do about it."

"Willy, what if it's drugs?"

"What do you mean?"

"My mom gets all these medical magazines and I look at them because I might become a doctor too one day. One of them had an article about how some drugs can cause these kinds of these things. What they call a psychotic break. And remember I told you Ben was hanging out with those druggie guys at school?"

"Wow, what would his dad say if that was what happened?"

"What a mess if it's drugs."

"Yeah, what are people at school saying?"

They had a long chat full of gossip and conversation. Lailla was still struggling with how to handle the girls at school who were bullying her, and they tried to figure out strategies to deal with them.

Then Willy's mom called her for supper and Lailla decided it was time to do homework.

But that night, lying in bed, Willy couldn't sleep at all. She knew Ben was out there somewhere. She could just feel it, could get some sense of his hurt and despair and confusion. But there was nothing she could do to help him.

The next day, Willy asked her mom to drive her to the stables earlier than usual. It wasn't her regular time to ride but she told her mother that Victoria had asked her to come over and help with the new horse. "We're trying to get her used to disabled riders." Willy said. "She's great but she's a little unsure of herself just now. Victoria figures it would be better if she started off with me rather than one of the kids."

All of which was true, Willy thought to herself. She wasn't lying, Except Victoria had said they would start next week, not today. But her mom was happy to drive her over there and agreed to come back in a couple of hours.

"What are you doing here?" Victoria asked.

"I thought I'd spend a little extra time with Sand. I was thinking I'd take him for a little walk along the river. It was so nice there yesterday."

"You're sure that's not too much for you?"

"I can manage if we go slow."

"And what if Sand decides to be an idiot?"

"He won't."

"Willy, I'm up to my ears here — hay delivery, stall cleaning and I'm short a volunteer. Look, just take him on the grass for a bit. You're right. That will be good for both of you. But no wandering off. Stay in the grassy field."

"I'm going to tack him up and do a bit of longeing too."

"Okay, but in the round pen, not in the field."

"Yes, ma'am."

Someone yelled from the back of the barn.

"Yes, be right there," Victoria yelled back and then hurried off.

Willy moved slowly and carefully, cane in one hand, as she got Sand out of his stall, cross-tied him and began to brush him. As always, she admired his deep rich chocolate-brown coat. His brown eyes shone with a gentle fire. As she brushed him, he turned his head, chewed on the flap of her coat pocket, rubbed his head against her and then licked her hand.

"Oh, you're a silly, silly old thing," she crooned, and bent to brush his legs. She spent time making sure his long mane and tail were free of knots and tangles. Finally, she got the bridle and saddle. With some trouble, she put them on, grabbed her cane and led him with her other hand on the reins. She glanced back down the hall just before she went out the wide door. Victoria was down at the far end of the hall with two men, helping them unload and stack bales of hay. It looked as if they would be busy for a while.

Now all she had to do was get on him, far enough away that Victoria wouldn't notice anything. She led him into one of the outdoor riding rings where there was a mounting block, manoeuvred Sand beside it, and then hoisted herself awkwardly into the saddle, reins in her hands. But she managed it and Sand stood still through the whole thing, although he shifted sideways a couple of times. She threw her cane behind the mounting block.

When she was on and organized, she gathered up the reins and urged Sand at a fast trot out the riding ring gate and then out of the alley between the field and the ring and out onto the path where she and Victoria had ridden yesterday. She pushed Sand into a fast trot and then a canter, and he took to it easily, with no sign of nervousness.

The place that Ben had showed her was only about a mile south of the riding centre, somewhat further than she had gone with Victoria the day before. She just had to get there. She had to check on Ben. If he was there, and if he saw it was her, he might come out of his hiding place and talk to her. Maybe she could persuade him to come back to the barn with her. Victoria was going to skin her when she found out what Willy was up to, but if she could help Ben in some way it was all worth it.

It seemed like no time had passed before she was at the place by the river. Sand had behaved perfectly so far. There was a thick grove of old fir trees and a path leading down from the park to the riverside. Willy urged Sand down the path; he didn't want to go, but eventually he placed his feet carefully down the rocky gullied path. At the bottom, there were several huge boulders leaning against one another, with sand and bits of driftwood around them. The rocks were too close together for Sand to get between them and Willy knew if she got off Sand here, she'd never be able to get back on him again, nor could she walk all the way back to the stables.

"Ben," she called softly. "Ben, it's me, Willy. I just want to talk to you. Ben, are you here?" She wondered if he could hear her over the sound of the rushing river. "Ben," she called again. "Ben, I know you're here somewhere. Come out. It's only me. I just want to talk. Sand is here too. He'd like to see you."

She waited, listened. Sand shifted uneasily underneath her. He didn't like this place.

Suddenly he reared, as someone in a black hoodie darted out from the rocks. "Go away, go away, leave me alone. Leave me alone!" Ben's voice! Then Ben scrambled over the rocks, ran into the water, and then when it was deep enough, he dived into the river.

"Ben! No!" Willy screamed. But Sand, startled, turned and bolted up the path to the top of the riverbank, and then took off in a mad gallop towards the stable. Willy almost fell, still holding the reins, but she grabbed his neck with both hands and hoisted herself back into the saddle. Then she hung on. It was all she could do. Sand was bolting back down the river-bank path. She yanked on the reins to no effect. Well, maybe heading for the stables was the best thing. Ben needed help and fast. The river wasn't that big but it was full of rapids and boulders and he would be swept downstream. Trying to swim a swiftly flowing, freezing-cold river was crazy. Crazy. Ben was crazy. She might as well admit it. He had been her friend once but the boy she had liked and admired was gone, disappeared into some kind of strange world where she couldn't follow. Instead of trying to stop Sand, she urged him forward, leaned on his neck, yelled, "Go, go."

He was racing at top speed. For now, she had to concentrate on staying on top of Sand. If she fell off when he was going at this speed, she'd be badly hurt, if not killed. And then, when they got to the stable, she had to make sure that Sand turned in the gate. She had to get him slowed down before they got there, somehow. She hoped, at this speed, he would get tired quickly.

She grabbed the reins tighter and slid her hands alternately forward, leaned over Sand's neck and pulled back on each rein, one at a time. Pull, release, pull, release. He slowed a bit. She tried it again, pull, pull, pull, pull, release. He slowed a bit more and she leaned back and braced both hands against his neck, braced her back and legs against the saddle. Pull, release. He responded, slowed again, finally, down to a trot and when they came to the gate, she was able to turn him into the lane leading to the stable door, and slow him to a walk. By now he was puffing and streaming with sweat.

But Victoria had heard the hoofbeats and met her at the door. "Willy, what are you doing? Where have you been?"

"It's Ben," Willy yelled. "He's in the river. Call 911. Hurry!"

"What?"

"Ben! He jumped in the river."

Victoria caught Sand's bridle. Willy kicked her feet out of the stirrups and slid off Sand's back. She hung onto Sand's saddle, breathing hard. Sand stood with his head down, also breathing in deep fast breaths.

"It's Ben," Willy said. "I found him. I called him. He freaked. He ran into the river. Call 911, Victoria, please! I've got Sand. I'm okay."

Victoria finally seemed to snap out of her shock. "Right," she snapped. "I'll deal with you later."

She pulled out her cell phone, started stabbing numbers. Willy leaned against Sand's sweaty side. He reached his head around as if to say he was sorry. She rubbed his head and scratched his neck. Steam billowed in clouds off his back and chest.

Victoria clicked off the phone. "The police are on their way. But they are going to need you to show them where to go. Give Sand to me. He's going to need to be walked so he can cool off. I'll clean him and put him away. And when this is done with, and Ben is safe, you and I need to talk. How could you do such a stupid thing! And where is your cane?"

Meekly, Willy handed over the reins, and Victoria stomped off leading Sand. When Sharlene brought her cane, Willy limped out to the parking lot. Her whole body was stiff and sore. But she hadn't fallen off. And she had brought Sand under control, all on her own. He had responded to her. Although she really didn't want to think about all the things that could have gone wrong. And she had found Ben. Who even now might be tumbling along the bottom of the river, his eyes open and his lungs full of water.

She jiggled and fidgeted and limped in circles until the RCMP cruiser pulled into the parking lot. Ben's dad jumped from the cruiser, followed by another officer.

He ran to her, grabbed her arm. "What happened? Where is my son? What did you do?"

"He's in the river," she said. "He jumped in when I called to him."

"When, how long ago?"

"I don't know, twenty minutes maybe?"

"Call Search and Rescue," Ben's dad snapped at the other man. "Hurry. You. Get in the car," he said to Willy. "Show us."

Siren wailing, lights flashing, the police car sped past all the traffic to the park, into the park entrance, and then across the grass to the trail where Willy and Sand had gone down to the river's edge. Willy got out of the car. "Down there," she said, pointing. The two men ran down the trail, leaving her behind.

But ten minutes later they returned. "No sign of him," Ben's dad said grimly. "But he was there. Or someone was there. There's some empty tin cans and an old blanket. Plus the remains of a fire."

"Search and Rescue is on its way here," the other cop said.

"No point in coming here," Ben's dad snapped. "If he's in the river, he's downstream somewhere. Or hiding in the brush. Tell them we need two boats and the chopper. And we need search crews to go along both sides of the river. Tell everyone to meet at the Lakewood Bridge ASAP."

"C'mon," he snapped at Willy again. "In the car. Hurry. On the way to the bridge, you can tell me what happened."

Instead, he sat up front, with the other officer, while Willy huddled, miserable and uncomfortable, in the back. Her legs hurt. The insides of them were rubbed raw, her back ached, and all she wanted was to go home and lie down. And also, somehow, know that Ben was safe. She shouldn't be worried about her own discomforts while Ben was fighting for his life, or possibly drowned, in the river.

And she also needed to explain herself to Ben's dad and to Victoria. It wasn't fair that everyone was mad at her. After all, she had found Ben, even if it hadn't turned out the way she expected. And she had stayed on Sand when he had gone crazy with fear and bolted for home.

They reached the bridge. A huge yellow Search and Rescue van was already there with its lights flashing; other vehicles were pulling up, and people were jumping out wearing yellow vests.

"Okay, everyone," Ben's dad yelled. "We're looking for a seventeen-year-old boy named Ben Morris. He's my son. We have a report that he ran into the river. He could still be in the river or he could be in the brush on either side of it. He's very frightened and trying to evade pursuit. If you see him, back off and call me immediately. I think I can help keep him calm. Whatever you do, don't scare him any more than you can help. Keep checking in with each other and with me. All right. Any questions?"

There were quite a few questions, and Ben's dad dealt with them calmly even though Willy could see his hands curled into fists at his side. His whole body was vibrating with impatience. After the questions were dealt with, everyone seemed eager to get going. The searchers were divided into four parties, two to go upriver on either side and two to go downriver. A rubber boat came roaring up the river with a team of divers in wetsuits. Ben's dad scrabbled down the bank to talk to them. Willy huddled on the bank beside the bridge. A cold wind had come up and she was hungry. And freezing. It was getting dark. Finally, the boat roared off and Ben's dad came back up the bank. For the first time, he seemed actually to look at her. Actually to see her. She was shaking with cold.

"Sorry," he said. "Get in the car and I'll turn on some heat."

They got into the front of the police car and Ben's dad turned on the motor. "Sorry," he said. "I was so worried about Ben I kind of forgot about you. Now what can you tell me? How did you know where to look? How did you get there? Tell me the whole story. All the details. Don't leave anything out."

"Ben showed me, last spring. He said this place was special. He said he liked to go down there to think about things. We went there when I was in a wheelchair so I didn't go right there but I knew where it was."

"And you rode down there on a horse? I thought you just said you were in a wheelchair."

"I used to be in a wheelchair. But Ben got me riding and that helped me walk again. Yeah, I rode my horse, Sand, down there from the Therapeutic Riding Centre. I thought Ben would listen to me. When I went to see him in the hospital, he talked to me. I thought we were still good friends. I thought maybe I could calm him down, and he would come back with me."

"So what happened? Did you see him?"

"He came running from behind some big rocks. He was yelling, something like get away from me, and then he dived into the river. Sand . . . well, he got scared and bolted so that was all I saw."

Ben's dad put his face in his hands then lifted in his head and stared out the window at the darkening sky. "Sorry," he said. "This has been an absolute nightmare. I couldn't figure out what was going on with Ben. His mom died when he was only four. We've moved around a lot. He's always had a hard time making friends. Too many schools. Too many strange people. We were up north for quite a while, and that was really hard. I thought this town would be a new beginning for us both."

"Yeah, he stopped talking to me, too, for a while. He was driving me to riding. We were going for coffee and stuff and then it all just stopped. What's wrong with him?"

"It's pretty hard to explain. I'm not sure and neither are his doctors. It is as if he's living in two realities right now. He's got voices in his head telling him some strange stuff. He thinks he's being followed. He thinks something or someone is out to get him. That's why he stole a car. He was trying to get away."

"Is he crazy?"

"I don't know. I can't really tell you anything."

"I'm so sorry," Willy said. "I'm sorry I scared him. I thought he might talk to me."

"It's not your fault. It's not anyone's fault. It's just one of those things that happens, and then you have to figure out how to deal with it."

"Like my car accident?"

"Is that what happened to you? Sorry, I didn't know."

"It's okay. The riding made me stronger. It made me strong enough to walk again. I owe it all to Ben. I owe him so much. When I met him, I was still so mad about the accident, I wouldn't talk to anyone and he helped me anyway."

"Willy, I'm taking you home and then I am going to join the search. We could be out here all night."

Willy hesitated. She said, "Will you call me? Please. When you know anything. I mean, when you find him."

"I'll be busy," he said. He looked at her face. "I'll try," he added.

He drove her home, walked her to the door, said hello to her mother and father, and then turned around, climbed in the police cruiser and screeched away, lights on and siren wailing.

Chapter 12

"WILLY, WILLY, WAKE UP." Her mom's voice in her ear. "Joe Morris just called. They found Ben. He's okay. He's back in the hospital. He has hypothermia and he's pretty banged up from some rocks in the river, but he's okay. Hear me?"

"Oh Mom." Willy's eyes snapped open. She sat up and threw her arms around her mother. "Oh Mom, I'm so glad."

"And Victoria called."

"Oh, oh."

"Yes, oh, oh is right. She's not too happy with you."

"I know. But Mom, you have to listen to my side. You need to hear the whole story."

"She says you took Sand out of the stable without telling

her, that you took him along the river, and he bolted with you on the way home. She says she has to rethink the whole deal. She has to consider whether you or Sand can stay there any more. She says you put the whole therapeutic riding program at risk."

"Yes, but I did it for Ben. I did it to find Ben. I couldn't walk there. I thought he would talk to me if I could only find him by myself. And yes, Sand bolted but he listened to me, he slowed down, he was only trotting by the time we got to the stable."

"Hmm. Well, Victoria's really, really mad, just the same. She says you could have been badly hurt. I don't know what we are going to do if you can't ride there anymore. I guess we will have to rethink the whole deal with Sand. There is no-where else to keep him."

"But I found Ben. How come no one has noticed that? How come no one has even thanked me?"

"Willy, you didn't think. You should have called someone. You should have called Ben's dad and let him know, let him go down there. What did you think you were doing? Yes, it was heroic; it was also stupid. If you'd fallen off Sand, you could have been re-injured, maybe paralyzed again, maybe killed. And Sand could have been hurt too, running crazy like that; he wouldn't know what he was doing. He could have run through a fence or out onto the highway again. And what about Victoria, after all she's done for you? This is how you treat her?"

"But I was just trying to help."

"Then help in the right way. Learn about what will really help Ben. Go talk to his counsellors. Find out what is wrong with him and take their advice as to what to do. Think, Willy."

"His dad said he was living in two realities, that Ben thought someone was after him all the time. That's why he ran away."

"Yes, he doesn't know who to trust right now. You can't talk to him the way you used to. You've got to accept that the Ben you knew is gone. Or rather, there are two Bens, the one you knew and this new Ben, who is living in a different world from the rest of us."

Willy turned around and fell back on the bed. Then she turned over and buried her face in her pillow. After a while, her mother got up and left the bedroom, and Willy heard the door close. She lay there for a long time. She heard water running, heard the phone ring. She could smell bacon cooking, hear her sister's voice, her mom and dad talking. She couldn't make out the words. She just felt so tired and sad. What would she do now if Victoria kicked her out of riding? What would she do if her parents didn't buy Sand? If she lost Sand? If he went to some other owner who didn't understand him? What if Sand ended up being put down because someone bought him who didn't understand him? It would be all her fault.

Some time later, her mom knocked on her door. "Willy, are you getting up today?"

"Yeah." But she didn't want to get up. She just curled up in the middle of the bed until the need to use the bathroom and get a drink of water drove her to her feet. When she looked in the mirror in the bathroom, she was shocked at what she saw: dark circles under her eyes, her hair dusty and wind-blown, her face pale. Her freckles stood out along her cheekbones. She had a shower, got dressed, went out to the kitchen and slumped into a chair. Her mom placed some toast and some hot chocolate in front of her then sat at the table across from her.

"Do you want to go to the stable today?"

"No," she said.

"But it's your lesson. Victoria will want to see you."

Willy sighed. "I don't even know if she's talking to me or not."

"Well, you have to deal with Victoria sooner or later. Somehow."

"I guess so." Tears trickled down her cheeks and dripped off her chin onto the table. She stared at the toast. The very thought of it stuck in her throat.

Finally, she dressed, and her mom drove her to the stables. Victoria stood at the open door of the stable, hands on hips, face a mask. "We'll talk after your ride," she said. Her mouth was a straight line, her gaze flat and direct. "You'll ride Kuna today."

"Fine," whispered Willy. She limped down the hallway be-tween the stalls to where Sand had his fine-boned head stuck out, calling to her and then whirling around to pace in his stall.

She went in the stall, took some time with him, scratched his chest and under his throat, felt his legs to make sure he hadn't damaged anything. He pushed at her with his head, plainly saying, "Come on, let's go out."

"Not today" she whispered to him, "but soon." She let herself out of his stall, went to get Kuna and help saddle him. When she was on his back in the ring, they did their warm-ups, walking, trotting, cantering in circles. Then Victoria brought out a series of orange cones. "We were supposed to videotape your actual dressage test today but that has to be postponed until you and I have had a talk. If we go ahead with it, we can send it in, and you will get a mark from the Canadian Therapeutic Riding Association. I know you've done dressage tests before but now we have to make sure everything is smooth and effortless. Balance and rhythm, Willy, balance and rhythm." She talked normally but she didn't really look at Willy.

For an hour they practised moving from a walk to a trot to a canter and then making the transitions back down again, coming to a full stop precisely where they were supposed to, with all of Kuna's feet in a nice square alignment. Finally, Victoria said, in her new toneless voice, "Good, that's enough for one day. Excellent work, Willy, you and Kuna are really coming along."

Willy slid off Kuna, took the reins to lead him in for

unsaddling. But once they were inside, Victoria said, "Let Elizabeth do the unsaddling today, Willy. We need to talk. Come to my office."

Willy had only been in Victoria's office once before. There were horse pictures, ribbons from long-ago horse shows and framed certificates on the walls. There was also a desk and a bookshelf full of books.

Victoria sat down and Willy sat in the chair in front of the desk. There was a long silence. Then Victoria sighed. "Willy, I was so mad yesterday that I was simply going to send you and Sand out of here. Ask you to leave immediately. I'm still thinking that would be the right thing to do. Almost anyone would agree with me. But I've had time to think. I do sort of understand why you did what you did and frankly, in your place, I might have done the same thing. I think it is admirable that you care so much about Ben. But you risked your life, you risked Sand's life, you risked the integrity and reputation of my business. In fact, you could have destroyed the Therapeutic Program here if you had fallen and been hurt. People would say it was my fault. Did you think about any of this?"

Willy was silent, thinking. Had she considered anything else but Ben? Not really. In fact, if she was really being honest with herself, she hadn't even thought of what might happen after she had found Ben. She had acted on impulse and had, very deliberately, not even considered the consequences. Because if she had considered them, she wouldn't have done it.

"No, I didn't. I just did it. I guess it seemed as though I could deal with everything else later."

"That's what I thought."

There was another long silence. "Willy, I saw you coming back. I saw you and Sand. I saw that he responded to you, he slowed down. Yes, he was tired but he was also listening. You did have him under control. He's a very bright horse and he was listening to you. And he's getting better, no question about it. I saw that too."

Willy stared at her. "Yes, he is. I told you that."

Victoria sighed. "Willy, did you learn anything yesterday? Did you think about what you did? Do you understand why I am so angry?"

Willy looked at the floor. "I thought about it all night. I didn't sleep. Please, please, Victoria, don't make us go. If I lose Sand, I don't know what I will do. If I lose Sand, I lose everything. And I did learn something. I learned two things: to think harder about what I'm doing before I do it, and to ask for help when I don't really know what I'm doing."

Victoria pressed her lips together.

"All right, I am going to let you stay, on probation. If there is any more trouble with Sand, that's it. Out he goes, and out you go. I am going to meet with your parents as well. And please, never, never give me an excuse to have to call you in here again unless it's to give you a first-place ribbon."

Willy walked out of Victoria's office with her heart heavy in her chest.

The next morning, Ben's dad rang their doorbell while Willy was sitting at the table eating toast with strawberry jam and drinking orange juice.

Willy's mom answered the door. "Mr. Morris?" she said.

"Please, call me Joe. May I come in? I need to talk to Willy."

"Yes, of course, come in. Can I offer you a cup of coffee or something?"

"Coffee would be great."

He sat down at the table. "Hey Willy, how are you?"

"Good. How is Ben?"

He put his face in his hands for a long moment then finally sat up. He rubbed both sides of his face. He looked tired enough to lie down on the table and go to sleep.

"Well, that is what I came to talk to you about. He seems to be feeling better and he is asking to see you. I came to see if you were up to it. And also, to thank you for all your help the other night. I was so upset myself I didn't even think about how you must have been feeling. Sorry about that."

"That's okay. I am just glad you found Ben and he wasn't, I mean, he hadn't . . ."

"Drowned? Yeah, me too." He paused. "Yep, that was pretty much the worst night of my life. We didn't find him until morning when it got light, and we could call in the dog squad." He leaned his head in his hands again. He hadn't shaved. Dark shadows underlined his eyes.

"Things will get better now. I just know they will," Willy said.

Joe was wearing his RCMP uniform and he had his hat tucked under his arm. When Willy's mom brought the coffee, he put his hat on the table and took a long sip.

"Mm, great coffee," he said. "A lot better than what we make at the station. Thanks."

Willy's mom put a plate of buttered toast beside his coffee. "There's fresh strawberry jam," she said. "This year's batch."

Joe helped himself to jam, gulped down the toast and coffee and then turned back to Willy.

"Boy, I was hungry. I forgot I hadn't eaten. That was great. Anyway, I can take you over to the hospital this morning if you want. But first, you need to talk to a counsellor so you can understand what Ben is going through. They think he might have something they call bipolar, but they're not really sure. And Willy," he hesitated, "he's on quite a few drugs so he might sound a bit funny. His speech is slow but he's making sense. He doesn't remember being in the river. I am glad about that."

"Okay, I'll just get changed."

"Sure, no problem."

In her room, Willy hurried to get dressed. Luckily, she had had a shower the night before. She threw on a pair of her favourite jeans, and a white t-shirt with a black hoodie over that. She grabbed her backpack with all her gear. Suddenly she stopped. Yes, she was nervous. Despite her brave words, she wasn't sure what she would be facing at the hospital. She still remembered all too vividly Ben's distorted white face as he ran out of the bush, screaming at her to get away. He had sounded as if he hated her, as if she were the most evil creature he could imagine. And then he had run into the river. Was he her friend? Why did he want to see her now? Did she really want to see him? She hesitated. They weren't even friends anymore. Or were they? The whole thing was so confusing.

This morning, she was stiff and needed both canes. She hobbled out of her room. "Ready," she said.

"Okay. Thanks for the coffee, Mrs. Cameron."

"No, no, call me Elizabeth, Liz for short."

"I'll bring Willy back later."

"Great, see you then. Willy, give our love to Ben from the whole family. Tell him to get well soon."

"Yes, I will."

This time in the police cruiser, Willy felt strange. The last time she had been too tired to notice how weird it was to be riding around town in a police car. She didn't know if she wanted people to notice her or not. She slunk down in the seat a little. But Ben's dad noticed and laughed.

"Want me to turn on the siren and lights?" he asked. "Ben would never get in this car with me. Said people would think he'd been arrested. Or if they knew he was a cop's kid, they'd think he was showing off."

"It's okay," she said.

At the hospital, Joe led the way inside and down a long, brightly lit hospital corridor to an office. Willy remembered all over again why she hated hospitals. Even though it had been a year and a half ago, she still remembered her terror on waking, unable to see, unable to move, not knowing where she was or even who she was. And look how far she had come since then. She was walking with a limp and two canes instead of her usual one, but still, walking.

Joe knocked on an office door, and then opened it for her. A young-looking man was sitting behind the desk. "This is Paul," he said, "Ben's counsellor. Paul, this is Willy."

Willy sat in the chair in front of the desk. Joe went out quietly, closing the door behind him.

"Willy, I understand you have been good friends with Ben. Can you tell me something about that?"

"We're just friends. Not like boyfriend, girlfriend or anything. We met at physio. He used to drive me to riding lessons. He seemed like a nice guy, then he changed."

"Right, can you remember when he changed, or why?"

"I remember it because it was so sudden. It was about the time I started walking. One day I walked out of the arena by myself, and he didn't talk to me all the way home. He didn't even say goodbye. Just dropped me off and left."

"How long ago was that?"

"Maybe last spring? I wrote about it in my journal. So what's wrong with Ben? Why did he change?"

"We're not sure. We've done a bunch of tests, but nothing has really shown up. He's had some kind of psychotic break but we don't really know why, and he's not telling us much.

But he does want to see you, so we think that is a good thing. He does seem to be reacting much more normally, eating, drinking and so on. I know he's had a couple of talks with his dad as well. I'll take you down there. Don't stay too long, keep the conversation light and normal. No big heavy questions about why he did what he did. He doesn't seem to remember his time in the river so probably just as well to stay away from that."

"Okay," Willy said.

She followed Paul down the long hallway to the elevator, up several floors, along another hall, to a room where he knocked on the door and then opened it. Ben was sitting on the side of the bed. His face lit up when he saw Willy.

"Hey, you came. I wasn't sure you would."

"Of course I came. I really wanted to see you. Been missing you at the horse barns. Nobody cleans poop as good as you."

"Yeah, I miss it. Miss the horses, miss riding. Miss driving you around."

"Yeah, now my poor mother has to drive me. She never complains. Sometimes I wish she would."

He went still for a moment. Then he said, softly, "Yeah, poor old parents. I guess I gave my dad a hard time. I don't really remember it."

Willy waited. Ben shook his head. Then he said, "Don't tell my dad this, okay?"

Willy nodded.

"I took some drugs, or a lot of drugs. I don't really know

what they were. A mix of stuff. I was feeling so bad, you know. Out of it. I just wanted to escape. Willy, I was just so lonely. I've been hanging around with these guys. I don't even like them much. You know, that druggie bunch that hangs out behind the auditorium."

"Yeah?"

"I've been so down. Feeling like I don't belong anywhere. We move so much. I can never make friends. I felt for a while like you were my first real friend. I'm not really good at friends. You know?"

"No, I don't know," Willy said. "We've never moved. I've been in the same house and the same town my whole life. My friends have been my friends, like, forever."

"Wow, really. I can't even begin to figure what that's like. With a nice mom and dad. Nice little sister."

"We're even getting a dog. Or two dogs. We decided to adopt the dogs we've been fostering."

Ben started to laugh. "Wow, too much. The perfect family."

"Until I was crippled."

"You're not crippled. You're walking and riding. I should probably hate your guts for being so perfect but I don't. I just feel . . . oh, I don't know what I feel."

He turned his head away and started to shake. "What did I do, Willy? No one will tell me anything. Did I kill someone? Wreck something? Break something?"

"No, nothing like that." Willy squirmed. "They told me not to talk to you about it."

"Why? Not knowing doesn't make me feel any better. I'd rather know so I can deal with it, at least apologize for doing whatever I did."

Willy hesitated. "You didn't hurt anyone. You stole a car. And you scared Sand and you jumped in the river."

Ben shook his head. "I have little bits of memories. Like flashes. But I can't tell which ones happened and which were hallucinations. I remember seeing you on a horse but I didn't think that was real. I thought you were some kind of ghost because some part of my brain remembered that you couldn't ride him. And he looked so huge and dark, like a monster. I thought he was going to run over me."

"He was just as scared of you."

"Yeah, I know that now. But I didn't then."

"Ben, why were you so lonely? I thought we were friends. And then you just disappeared out of my life. I didn't understand. I still don't."

"Willy," Ben's voice faltered. "I'm so sorry. I'm so sorry. You seemed so fine. So happy. What did you need me for? I was afraid I would just drag you down with me."

"Ben, you saved my life, do you know that? I owe you so much. When you met me I was mostly just sitting around feeling sorry for myself. Talking me into going to therapeutic riding got me out of the wheelchair, but more than that, it gave me something to live for, something to do, something to care about. I owe you. How could you drag me down anywhere?"

"Because you were important to me. I was afraid of losing you."

"So you ran away before that could happen?"

"Yeah, guess so."

They were both silent.

"So what do we do now?" Willy asked. "Are we friends? Are you just going to run away again? When you say I'm important to you, what does that mean? You know, Ben, I lost a bunch of friends too, people I thought I could count on, people from school. They all came *once* to visit me, after the accident and stood around looking uncomfortable, and then I didn't see them again. That's why I don't want to go back to school. I don't want to have to face them. What do I say? Oh hello, ex-buddies, dear friends. Thanks for your support?"

"I didn't know that."

"Lailla stuck by me, and I left her in school to face being bullied all by herself. Yet she's still my friend. She always will be. And I will always be her friend no matter what happens in our lives. So yeah, people that stick with you are worth keeping."

Willy went over to the window and looked out. Far away below the hospital she could see the black water of the river. This section of the river was lined by sharp rocks and steep cliffs. She turned around and looked back at the small cell-like room.

"Ben, you need to decide who your real friends are. A real friend sticks around no matter what. I want to be your friend.

I will be if I can, if you'll let me. My whole life is changing for the better. I think you should get better and then you should come back to riding. I think that would be absolutely the best thing you could do right now for yourself. Maybe I'll see you there. I'm here for you. I always will be. I'll see you soon, okay."

She was going to cry and she didn't want to cry in front of Ben. So, after such a grand speech, she turned and left. She didn't slam the door, just closed it gently behind her, walked down the long hall, and as she walked, she pulled out her phone and texted Lailla.

"Hey, where are you?"

"Home," Lailla texted. "Homework. That's what I do. Homework. Study. Nerd girl you know."

Willy dialled her cell number and Lailla said, "Yes, Willy. What's up?"

"Meet me at my place." Willy said. "I have no idea what to wear."

Lailla laughed. "Ha, I knew it. You are so on the way back to school. The school nasties will be running for their lives. You are so coming back to school in January."

"Yes, but I still limp."

"You can hardly see it."

"I use a cane. Some days two canes."

"So, what is the big deal about that. Just look them in the eye. And then maybe trip them a bit with your canes. Just a little bit."

"Nope. I've got a plan. Just ignore them. Did you know the

word sand means tough? Well, I am going to imitate my horse. Got sand, baby, sand. I'm going to go in the door and sail down the hall with my canes. As in who cares what anyone thinks. As long as I have the right shoes, of course, and the right jeans and the right shirt. The very latest. So meet me at my house, immediately, old pal. Because if I don't have the right clothes, and I am pretty sure I do not, that means you, and me, and mom, and her credit card are all going shopping!"

But as she limped down the hall, the conversation with Ben went round and round in her head. Did she mean what she had said? Would she really be there for him? It felt as if she had made a big decision. Too big. She didn't know this new Ben that well. What if he never got better? What if the not-Ben part of him was always there, talking too fast, taking medical drugs to slow him down and connect him with reality? Did she really want to be there for him or had she just committed herself to a promise she couldn't keep?

She phoned her mother to come and pick her up. She waited in the hospital lobby watching people come and go, shivering as gusts of cold air hit her as the doors slid open and then closed and then opened again. She went outside when she saw her mother's car, glad to be away from the hospital, and away from Ben.

Lailla was waiting for her, sitting on the doorstep of their house. They went into Willy's room, giggled over clothes and gossip from school. Willy didn't mention her conversation with Ben, and Lailla didn't ask.

Chapter 13

"BEN IS HOME AND he's going to start school again," Willy said to Lailla on the phone. "He wants me to meet him at the park. You have to come with me. Please. I haven't talked to him for a month. I promised I would, then I just got so busy with school and riding, and now I feel guilty."

"I thought you two were friends again."

"Yeah, sort of. I just don't know who he is anymore. It makes me so nervous. I promised to be his friend, and then I didn't even call him. I feel like such a jerk."

"I don't know him either. I've never met the dude."

"Then it's time you did."

"I don't really want to meet him, Willy. He sounds a bit scary."

"He's not. Please. Just come with me. We'll get ice creams. We'll sit in the park."

"It's January. It's freezing."

"Hot chocolate then."

"Okay." Lailla sighed.

Willy's mom dropped them off at the park and they walked to the bench where Ben was sitting.

"Hey, Willy," he said, "nice to see you." His smile lit up his face.

"Hey, Ben, this is my best friend, Lailla. Lailla, this is Ben. I thought it was about time you two met each other."

"Hey, Ben," Lailla said.

"Hi Lailla, nice to see you. I recognize you from school."

They all sat on the bench and stared awkwardly at the river. "It's too cold here," Willy said. "Let's walk up to King-fisher's and get some hot chocolate."

"Right," said the others together. They all laughed nervously.

But the walking didn't loosen things up nor did sitting in Kingfisher Books and Coffee, a favourite hangout, with mugs of hot chocolate topped with whipped cream in front of them.

"So Ben, when are you starting school?" Willy finally asked.

"I don't know," he said. "But I have to go back. I have to catch up and finish grade twelve. But how do I face everyone? I still don't even remember what happened. Sorry. That's why I needed to see you. I needed to talk about it. You're back at school, right?"

"Yes, I am," Willy said. "It's not easy. Some people are friendly. Some people don't look at me. But everybody does this weird thing, even the teachers. They say, how are you, and then they don't wait for an answer. They just say, oh you're looking so good, and they march off. Somehow that is supposed to make me feel better about myself, I guess. I limp along on two canes but I look good doing it."

"You do look good," Lailla said. "You're blonde, you're gorgeous. When I got all my hair cut off, everyone said, oh, you got your hair cut. No one said whether it looked good or terrible."

"You look great," Willy said.

"At least they talk to you," Ben said. "I have counsellors. They talk *at* me."

"I'm sorry I didn't call, Ben," Willy said softly.

"It's okay. I needed time to sort myself out. I'm good. I'm off all the meds. I feel like myself. I just don't know how to go back to school and face everyone."

"Are you coming back to riding?" Willy asked.

"I'd like to. Would Victoria have me back? I feel as if I let her down, too. I thought maybe she'd never talk to me again."

"Of course she wants you back. You were a good rider and great with the horses."

There was silence at the table. Then Willy laughed. "Just look at us," she said. "I'm crippled. Lailla, you're brown, and Ben, you're the crazy guy. We're the outsiders. And we're none of those things. Lailla, you're the brilliant doctor, Ben, you're the kind, caring man who is going to make a difference in the world, and me . . ."

"You're the blonde athlete princess," Lailla said, "who is gonna kick butt at the Olympics. I say we walk in the door of the school together, laugh our heads off, have a good time and face them all down. We know who we are and that's all we need. Ben, are you with us?"

He looked at them both. He put his head in his hands. He lifted his head, turned red and stared at them both. Then he smiled. "Yes," he said. "Yes, I am. Thanks, you guys."

■

"Okay," Victoria said briskly. "I think your probation time is over. Here's the new plan. Willy, every day I want you to spend some time with Sand. Halter him, put him in the round pen and do some longeing and other exercises. Walk with him. Make him stay right by your shoulder. Do lots of turns and circles. What we are going to do is rebuild his confidence step by step. We're going to go right back to basics and then you can start riding him again. I think you are right. He will be an amazing dressage horse, and you two will go to the top. Now that you have won first place in the video contest on Kuna, we can consider doing a video with Sand and then we can send that into the para-equestrian competition."

"That sounds great," Willy said.

"Once the basics are in place, you and Sand are going to

start some serious training, young lady. Judy is coming again to have a look at you both. Are you ready for that?"

"Yes, I sure am!"

"Okay, let's do it. And you, Ben, I have a new project for you. Come with me."

They followed her out of the room, down the long hall, and out into the back of the riding ring. An overweight red mare was standing in a pen, in a corner with her back to them. She turned her head to look at them and then crowded further into the fence.

"This is Fanny Mae," Victoria said. "A friend of mine found her a couple of days ago. She was out in a big field with a lot of other horses at Q Ranch. Someone brought her there as a boarder and then abandoned her, never paid a cent. The ranch owners have just been letting her hang out with their horses, but her feet were in terrible shape. She was lame, in pain, and couldn't walk much. So she just stood and ate and got fat. They were about to send her to the auction; that would have been the end of her."

Ben put his hand through the bars but the mare wouldn't even look at him.

"She doesn't like or trust people at all," Victoria added. "Plus she just got hauled here in a trailer. Then Robin, the farrier, had to tie her down to do her feet. So she's trauma-tized from all that. We think she might have been beaten up by a previous owner; that is why she is so mistrustful. So what I want you to do now, Ben, is go in the pen, and see if you can get her to move around just a bit. Don't go close.

Don't push her. Just aim your body at her hips, very easy and calm, and she will move away and start to circle around and then see if she will eventually turn and make some kind of connection with you. It's called join-up."

Ben opened the gate and slid quietly inside the pen. The mare's head went up. As soon as Ben took a step towards her, she whirled and ran around and around the pen. Another step and she ran again. Ben looked at Victoria.

"That's great, Ben. Just keep that pace, very slow, non-threatening. Just push her a bit more. Stop whenever she stops. Then push again. Her reward is that you stop when she stops."

This time the mare only ran at a fast trot, head raised and tail high. When she stopped, and Ben stopped, she dropped her head and sniffed the ground. Then she raised her head but flicked her ears back and forth.

"Good," Victoria called. "She's watching you. Now, just another step."

This time the mare moved away but just at a slow trot, head up, tail high and swishing. Ben just kept circling slowly behind her. Finally she stopped in front of him and turned to look at him.

"See how her ears are pointed towards you. Now reach out, let her smell your hand, and scratch her neck, very gently." Ben put a hand gently on the mare, started to scratch and stroke her fuzzy red coat. She threw her head up but didn't move. Instead she turned her head to watch him.

"Now just keep scratching and rubbing. Move slowly

towards her shoulder but don't try to touch her head. Let her sniff you if she wants. Just keep rubbing and scratching."

Eventually, Ben got as far as her shoulder. The mare reached her head around and sniffed at his shirt.

"Okay, that's good," Victoria said. "Give her a last scratch, no patting. She thinks patting is hitting. Now come out of the pen. Use your voice. Walk away slowly. Tell her what a good girl she has been. We'll do it all over again tomorrow. She's so lonely that she will soon start to see you as her friend instead of an enemy. Tomorrow you can try with some treats, apples and carrots. Once she starts seeing you as a friend, you can start working with her every day. Just little bits. Go slow, and take your time. Once she starts to trust you, then you can really change her view of the world. Instead of it being full of enemies, it will be full of friends and good things like brushing and apples."

"That is so amazing." Willy said. "She changed so much in just a few minutes."

"Wow," Ben said. "Wow, I changed too. I could feel it, when she looked at me. Some kind of connection. I'm not even sure what I felt. It was like we just really clicked."

"That is so cool," Willy said. "Wow, Ben, you are the horse-whisperer dude. I can see it. She just got you right away."

"Look you two," Victoria snapped. "This is all great and fun but I've got a business to run, students to manage, and people to deal with. I am not a horse rescue service. As of this moment, you two can start working off some of what it cost me to rescue and feed that freeloader mare. It'll take months to find a good home for her and in the meantime, there's poop to shovel, floors to sweep, horses to feed and brush. See you later."

She stomped off. Willy and Ben looked at each other and burst into laughter.

Victoria heard them laughing, started to turn, then straightened her shoulders and stomped even harder.

Willy grabbed a broom from where it was standing in the corner. "I'll sweep the hay dust. You scoop the poop," she said. "Meet you back here in an hour or so. And then I'm taking you out for ice cream. It's on me."

"Right," said Ben. He gave her a huge grin, and went down the hall, whistling softly to himself.

They met an hour later, stiff, sore and dusty, outside the arena. "Shower time," grinned Willy. She was leaning on both her canes, which she only did now when she was really tired.

"Ice cream first."

"Looking like this?"

"Let's get it to go, and then sit in the park."

It was a sunny Saturday in May, and Willy couldn't see any trace of the not-Ben she had encountered in the hospital except on occasional moments when he was tired, or his attention or focus wandered. Right now, he was staring at the river with his face twisted in pain.

"Sometimes, I can sort of remember it," he said. "I hit my head pretty good on a rock, my dad says. In addition to the drugs. No wonder I was so out of it."

"Yep, you were," Willy said cheerfully.

He turned and looked at her. For a moment, a strange person stared out of his eyes. "Willy, there's nothing scarier than not knowing what's real and what isn't. I didn't know what or who to trust anymore. It was like the whole world dissolved in front of me. I thought being dead would be easier. I thought if I were dead maybe I could go find my mom. That's all I really wanted. I missed her so much. That's why I stole the car, to go look for my mom."

He shivered and put his head in his hands.

"Don't think about it," Willy said, alarmed. "It's okay. We're here. I'm here. You can rely on me. I'm real. Eat your ice cream. It's real. Just taste it."

"It's okay. I'm okay. Sometimes it just comes back."

"Yeah, I know. And you know I know. That's why the red mare connected with you. She knew you understood her. But the bad stuff was a while ago; you're here now and everything is fine. It's good."

"My dad and I are doing so much better, Willy. He's different. We're going to counselling together and he even came to the riding centre to watch me ride." Willy nodded. He was friendly to Willy as well. If he was home, when Willy and Ben were studying together, he would order pizza and sit with them while they ate, trying to make conversation. He wasn't very good at it but he was getting better.

They ate their ice cream in the sun. The sun was warm and the wind was cold. The sun shone on the black-blue wrinkles of the river.

"Best friends," said Willy. "Remember?"

"Yeah," said Ben. "True. Willy, you didn't leave. You stayed with me when I needed you."

"We rescued each other, dude. We owe each other."

They looked at each other, smiled, deep and happy, sitting together watching the sun crinkle the river's surface silver.

AUTHOR'S NOTE

Although the people and events in this book are imaginary, it is true that many people are helped by therapeutic riding programs. People are helped both physically, by riding, and emotionally and psychologically, by connecting with the horses. People ride for therapeutic reasons, but some people with disabilities also compete as para-equestrian athletes. Some compete internationally. Canada's para-equestrian team has won many international championships and Olympic para-equestrian medals.

I began riding several years ago in order to get help for my rheumatoid arthritis. At first my joints and muscles were stiff, and I was terrified of falling off. But I had started riding when I was a child, and I had a lot of "muscle memory" that helped me remember how to ride. I overcame my fear quickly and began to take great joy and pleasure in riding. Eventually, my riding coach asked me if I wanted to try competing as a para-equestrian. My sister, who is a horse trainer, found me a horse, and now I compete as a para-equestrian through an organization called the Canadian National Therapeutic Riding Association (CANTRA). I ride in a sport called "dressage," which is a little bit like doing ballet with horses. The rider and the horse must do precise, controlled patterns and movements. Onlookers should not be able to see the cues that the rider is giving the horse. To do this well takes training and concentration, but for me, it has had the side effect of also helping my arthritis, and giving me the companionship of my horse, Caraigh. Caraigh was rescued by my sister from a situation where he was being starved and ignored. Now he works as a therapeutic riding horse and gets much attention and great food. He is one happy horse.

I am grateful to all the people who have helped with my riding and with training Caraigh. We are both still learning and have far to go but that means we have much to look forward to. Who knows what lies in our future? In the meantime, we enjoy what we do, and we appreciate the caring people as well as the great horses with whom we spend our time.

ABOUT THE AUTHOR

Luanne Armstrong has published nineteen books of fiction, nonfiction and poetry as well as many books for younger readers. Her books have been nominated for the BC Book Prizes, Red Cedar Awards, Silver Birch Awards, the Chocolate Lily Awards and many others. Her most recently published children's book was *Morven and the Horse Clan* (2013). She presently lives on her organic farm on Kootenay Lake, and her horse, Caraigh, works as a therapy horse at a therapeutic riding centre. Luanne and Caraigh compete in dressage nationally through the Canadian Therapeutic Riding Association.